BETWEEN
LIGHT
and DARK

BETWEEN
LIGHT
and DARK

RIAN MCMURTRY

ARPress
45 Dan Road Suite 36
Canton MA 02021

Hotline: 1(800) 220-7660
Fax: 1(855) 752-6001

Ordering Information:
Quantity sales. Special discounts are available on quantity purchases by corporations, associations, and others. For details, contact the publisher at the address above.

Printed in the United States of America.

ISBN-13:   Paperback   979-8-89676-213-3
                eBook   979-8-89676-214-0
                Hardback   979-8-89676-215-7

Library of Congress Control Number: 2024925149

For Karen.
Yes, I still remember you.

Running down the field, Angela looked over her shoulder, Johnny charging after her, his determination to catch her all over his face. The late afternoon August sun beat down the scattered clouds offering little respite from the glare and the heat. She slowed a little, one eye on Johnny behind her, and raised her arms to catch the ball as Alex dropped it right between the numbers on her uniform. She stuck her tongue out at Johnny and sped up. The white lines fell behind her… and just a bit more… the last one… Johnny leapt for her, and she felt his weight crashing into her back even as the whistle blew.

"Nice hustle Angie! Johnny good effort but she still scored," Coach Nguyen called.

"Yeah, so you can like get up now," Angela said.

"Sorry, Ange," Johnny said. When he'd stood up he offered his hand to her. He was shaking the other hand.

"You OK?" she asked.

"Yeah, don't worry. Your foot hit my hand while I was tackling you. No biggie." He smiled at her. "I didn't think you were that fast." He kicked some dirt off his cleats, and said, "We're totally ready for White Hill Christian."

Angela looked at him skeptically. "Coach, are we even going to have that game? I know it's the opening game of the season, but Reverend

Johnson's been whining a lot about me even being on the JV team, much less playing against his Neanderthals."

Coach Nguyen smiled at her. "Well, Fujimori, they complained about Jessie Blaylock for four years, and never actually cancelled a game despite her being a linebacker tackling their players. And this year there's Danielle Serafini, too." He paused, and she nodded; Danielle was a big girl, and was playing safety. He nodded over at the blond girl who trotted over. Two girls on the JV football team might be unusual-- there weren't enough girls to form their own team, let alone league—but half the freshman class turned out to watch practices and cheer on the JV squad. A different half each time, too. The PTA had arranged for school buses to take the kids back and forth, paying the drivers overtime.

But the first game of the year was against White Hill Christian Academy. No one seemed to know where they'd come from, but they practiced a strict religion. They'd taken over one of the old hill camps and transformed it. According to the San Rafael Bugler, students stayed up there during the week and came back on weekends to be with their parents. Which was really weird. Summer camp was one thing, but every week? Stuck with people like that crazy Reverend Johnson? Who'd really want that? But apparently they had enough people for a football team, all boys.

Lucas Valley High, on the other hand, was a public school. Admittedly, a public school with a wealthy and involved PTA. It was still a public school. The school had held open tryouts, and Danielle and Angela had made the JV team. There were a few other girls on teams scattered around the other local high schools. Now it was late August, Labor Day was fast approaching, and with it the first game of the year. And Angela felt like she was ready.

"Just remember, everyone. Make sure you keep your grades up! Anyone gets less than a C on a test and they sit next game. Anyone drops below a C average and they're off the team. Ms. Lee is very strict about that, and it's a good thing." The principal wasn't the only strict one. The PTA had gotten a coach fired for trying to keep failing students on the team. "I think that'll do it for today; I see the parents circling. Go get showered and changed. I'll see you in the game room tomorrow for film and review." Angela and Dani followed their teammates towards the locker rooms, peeled off for the girls' room (usually used by the volleyball, softball, and soccer teams, but they had lockers there, too). The hot shower would feel good.

Angela and Dani came out of the locker room to see the last bus waiting under the outer oaks. Coach was talking to Alex, Jeremy, and some of the other guys while Seth Dupree sat on the bus with his head down. Seth wasn't on the team; he was just a friend of Alex's, a sort of creepy goth. Alex Menendez certainly cleaned up nice. Neatly trimmed black hair, a tight T-shirt, shorts in the late summer afternoon. Even at fourteen, he was filling out with muscle. Not that the other guys weren't, but there was just something about Alex that made him so much more interesting than the other boys. His smile, the way he laughed… something. She knew she wasn't the only girl who thought so; Danielle was right there with her, and there were at least four girls—Dawn, Bridget, Keisha, and Jennifer--in that group of friends that he often hung out with. Oh, why was she obsessing about him anyway?

They walked together across the small parking lot. Teachers and staff had assigned spaces, and there was a chain to the outdoor basketball courts and blacktop where additional people could park for big events. Other than that it was a bus and bike place; even if Angela was old enough for a car, students couldn't park at the high school. All the streets around were ticket breeding grounds for everyone who wasn't a resident.

The bus was yellow of course, and had Lucas Valley High School in black letters. Edie Stoddard drove the bus today, she was in her early fifties, with gray hair. Friendly but she expected the kids on the bus to behave themselves. Last time there had been a fight the ex-Marine sergeant had come back and broken it up quickly. No one wanted her stopping the bus and coming back there. The seats were olive drab vinyl, the floor was black. In all, a school bus.

"Hi Ms. Edie!" Angela said as she boarded the bus.

"Hi Angela. Did you have a good practice?"

"Aye aye!" she responded.

"Good! Take your seat," Edie said, and then raised her voice, "If the slackers will get on board we'll get underway and get all you home!"

"What?" said Mike Wu. "Oh, sorry, Miz Edie!"

Angela waived good-bye to Jeremy Padover, one of her last good friends on the bus. Only she, Alex, and Seth were left. Seth was across from her, reading a book. Alex was talking on his cell phone—to his parents, it sounded like, talking about practice, and sipping on that sports drink syrup sludge he liked so much. She was bored, so she turned to Seth. "Whatcha reading?" He didn't respond, just kept reading and swigging from his sarsaparilla. She wasn't used to being ignored. "Hey, Seth, what are you reading?" He looked up, surprised.

"You're actually talking to me?" he said, the book still sitting in his lap.

"Um, yeah, you're the only other person here. Why are you so surprised?" It wasn't that strange.

"The only thing you usually say to me is "Go away"," he replied, returning his gaze to his book. He still hadn't shown her what he was reading, although it's hard cover made it look more like a textbook than the novel she'd presumed. Maybe it was a library book?

"Really? Sorry about that, " she said. She wasn't really. Seth wasn't one of her favorite people to begin with; his gothy mcgoth clothes, that weird miniflashlight he always had, his guyliner. But he was a friend of Alex's so she should probably make an effort, at least to be polite. "But I am still wondering what you're reading."

He flipped up the front cover. "Mummification Ritual in Egypt and the Andes".

"Ugh, gross. Why are you reading something like that? You can't have a paper due yet!"

He shrugged. "Death is my domain."

"Seth, can you BE more pretentious?" Alex interjected, and then he apologized to his mother and returned his attention to the phone.

"Of course I can be more pretentious, my good man. What ever made you believe such was beyond my capabilities?" Seth replied in a mock-English accent.

"Alex, did you HAVE to encourage him?" Seth's attention returned to her as he looked earnestly at her, clasping his hands in front of him.

"Only he can be more pretentious than I, good lady. Why, once..." Alex threw an eraser at him. Seth caught it inches from his face. Seth's attention shifted back to Alex. "Really, my good man, your skills as a quarterback are sadly lacking this lovely afternoon! I realize I hardly have the numbers the lady does for you to put your projectile between, but for a man in your position you should be at least somewhat more accurate!"

"I'd better not have to come back there!" the bus driver interjected.

"No, Ms. Edie!" they chorused. Seth returned his attention to his book, Alex went back to his phone, and Angela pulled a game device out of her bag. Soon she was lost in the beeping of her adventures in fantasy world and paying no attention to the world around her anymore. Then the bus hit something, swerved violently to the left, and started falling. She flew to the side, then back, before a pain in her head and then nothing more.

CHAPTER

2

A ngela woke suddenly, feeling someone's hands on her. The hands were cold, almost frozen where they rested on her head and chest… "Let go of me!"

"My apologies." Seth withdrew his hands from her head and under her clothes.

"How… How's your head, Ange?" Alex asked in a pain-soaked voice. She turned her head, and then Alex said, "No, don't move quite yet. You were out for a while. I'd guess you hit your head. Seth's the only one of us who came through OK." Alex's window was shattered and there was a piece of tree branch sticking in through it. There was a thick, heavy branch across Alex's lap, and it had quite a bit of blood on it. Seth, unfortunately, looked sweaty but otherwise fine.

"Keep him away from me, Alex. He had his hand down my shirt!" She wasn't moving, as Alex suggested, but was vaguely aware that Seth was around somewhere. She could smell him.

For that matter, everything seemed more intense. The freshly washed, clean scent of Alex. The unwashed, sweaty, stink of Seth, the blood, the stinks and smells left behind by kids on the bus, water from the creek, the biodiesel of the bus, the drab olive faux leather seats of the bus and the bare metal holding them in place. The gum under the seats. The pain in the back of her head and at her neck, the still chilled feeling on her forehead and chest, the…

"Miz Edie's dead. The sun visor cut through her skull. And my phone's toast. Either of you have one?" Seth returned to the conversation. He seemed remarkably calm, not even gloating about touching her. Well, maybe boys only did that when they were alone. For someone with such cold hands, his face was remarkably sweaty.

"Eww, gross."

"It's not pretty. But do either of you have a cell phone? We need to get an ambulance or something out here. You're both hurt."

"Seth…" Alex started. Seth looked at him, and even from the floor Angela thought that some sort of communication passed between them as they locked eyes and one of Seth's eyebrows rose. Almost as if Seth were saying Alex was in no shape to care for anyone, Angela didn't know how, and Seth himself wouldn't be able to. Which made no sense. Alex sighed. "Yeah, you're right. Ambulance it is. My phone is somewhere up towards the front of the bus. Ange?" He turned towards her and she could see the bloody mess of his face and arm. Absurdly, she wondered about his ability to play first of all.

"Um, it's in my backpack, I'll get it!" Angela got up a little gingerly, but she was feeling fine. A slight ache in her head and chest, a pain on her neck, but that was it.

"Ange, after that hit to the head, I don't think you should be getting up. Seth's fine; let him get it," Alex said.

"He's not going through my stuff, too, Alex!" she hissed at him. "I'll get my own phone! Seth can go do whatever goths do in the woods."

"We're in the creek bed, actually," Seth noted mildly. "I'm right here, you know. I can hear you perfectly well." He shuffled over towards Alex a bit. "If you'd rather make the call, be my guest. Alex, where did you throw yours? I'll go get that one in case there's something wrong with hers."

"Over there somewhere." He gestured towards the front of the bus.

"Are you sure you're a quarterback? First the eraser, now your phone? You don't know where you threw the pass?" Well, at least the insults were normal.

"Very funny, Seth." Some of the pain was gone from his voice, but Alex was clearly still hurting from all the cuts and scrapes he'd gotten when that window shattered. Seth moved carefully down the aisle. While Angela was digging in her backpack for her phone, she though she heard Seth mutter something. As she pulled it out she saw him down on his hands and knees picking something up. That was fast finding the phone. She hit the 911 and settled to handle the call. "911, what's your emergency?"

"Hi, our bus crashed on the way back from practice. The driver's dead, Alex is cut up, and I think I took a hit to my head. Seth seems to be fine." She was babbling a bit.

"Ok, Ma'am. Do you know what street you were on?"

"Lucas Valley Road. We're in the creek. We'd just passed a stop."

"What kind of bus is it?"

"School bus. Lucas Valley High."

"OK, do you know what your last stop was?"

"No. I mean, I know it's the one two before mine, but not the name of it or anything, and I don't know anything about where it was supposed to go after mine."

"Alright, keep your phone on and we'll try to coordinate its location. You mentioned injuries. Let's start with you. Where are you hurt?"

"Um the back of my head. I think I'm bleeding there some; it's wet and sticky."

"Are you experiencing any slurring of speech? Loss of memory?"

"Alex, am I slurring when I talk?"

"No," he replied. "You sound fine."

"I heard that," said the operator. "We'll get you checked out even so. Head injuries are nothing to take lightly. Do you have any other injuries?"

"A few scrapes and pains, but I think most of that is from practice."

"Ok, let's move on to your friends," she said.

"Seth isn't my friend. He had his hands on me when I was blacked out."

"You blacked out?" she said, typing furiously.

"Yeah. Alex looks like he's got a lot of small cuts and bruises that ripped his shirt and shorts something awful, but I think that's it. Alex, anything worse?"

"No, I think that's it." A snort came from Seth, who was now rummaging around back by the driver's seat.

"Ah, found it!"

"And the other person? Seth, you said his name was?"

"Oh, he's fine. He just got the first aid kit from up by the driver's seat."

"And you said that the driver is dead?" the operator asked.

"Yes Ma'am."

Seth had the first aid kit opened and he was starting to open an alcohol swab. "Alex, you know the tune so sing along."

"This is going to sting a bit!" they chorused.

"How do you know the driver is dead?" the operator wanted to know.

"Seth said the driver's visor went through her skull," Angela replied.

"Ok. You've been very helpful. You said that Seth was fine; can I talk to him, please?" she asked. "I'd like to get a bit more information from the only conscious and uninjured person present."

"I'd really rather he didn't touch my phone,"

"Put it on speaker," Seth suggested as he continued to daub at Alex's injuries with the alcohol. He'd discarded some of them already. "Or if you like you could hand me the phone and you can do this. It doesn't matter to me; this reckless idiot's bled on me before."

"Hey! Watch who you're calling an idiot! Do you want the whole team after you?" Alex protested, grinning

She made a face at Seth, but hit the speaker app.

Seth responded to Alex with a smile. "If the whole team wants it's usual electrolyte filled sports drink replaced with a powerful laxative, be my guest. Yes, Operator?"

"Seth, can you describe the driver's injuries?"

"From what I could see, "injury", singular. The visor struck her skull hard enough to penetrate and remove the upper three centimeters of the cortex, which are now on the floor of the bus behind her seat. She died on impact."

"Can you take a look at the back of Angela's head and describe the injury to me?"

He handed an alcohol swab to her and stepped around her. "Externally, it's a contusion approximately eight centimeters in diameter. Without some sort of medical equipment I couldn't say anything about the shape of her brain. The bleeding appears to have stopped."

"It's still wet, though."

"The seepage appears to have stopped. I could be wrong, of course. Do you want me to put a bandage on it?"

"No, I'll wait for the professionals."

"Ok. Your head, your blood." He moved back around her.

"Ange, come on. You could get an infection," Alex said. "I've certainly gotten enough when I haven't treated injuries quickly enough."

"I wouldn't bet on it, Alex," Seth put in, cocking an eyebrow at Alex.

"Not that I trust him, but the experts will be here sooner or later. I can wait."

"Then let me do it." She again got the impression that Alex and Seth were communicating with each other without speaking, and then Seth shrugged.

"Whatever. Alex, do you want me to see about getting this tree off you? Or do you want to wait, too?" Seth said.

"Right, like you can move it," Angela put in as Alex wiped the back of her head with a swab and then put a gauze pad on it.

"Can you hand me a roll?" he asked. She reached into the first aid kit and handed Alex a roll of gauze. "And, Seth, are you sure?"

"I can give it a try. Let me..." He fell silent, took a series of deep breaths.

"I should help..." Angela said.

"Don't move your head," Alex replied. "He'll use the windowsill for leverage."

Seth strained to lift the branch, but not as much as Angela expected, and soon had the branch off of Alex and out through the window. Angela was astonished at the feat of strength. "Thanks for the assist, Alex," he said.

With the injuries treated, they had little to do until the rescuers got there. At Alex's suggestion, she lay back down, cushioned her head and elevated her feet. Alex and Seth engaged in some quiet, serious conversation. She couldn't make out what they were saying but both boys were being very grim, and it seemed Alex's grimness wasn't a product of his injuries. She couldn't tell what caused it. When she tried to get close enough to understand what they were saying, she heard them talking about vacations and role-playing games.

The fire department pulled them out of the creek bed, with its low flow of water, rounded rocks, and steep earth embankments. Once they got the three of them out, EMTs began checking each of them out. Seth was given a once over and went to talk to the sheriff's deputies. The EMTs had her and Alex in an ambulance and prepared to take them to Marin General. When they were left alone for a few minutes, she asked him what he and Seth had been discussing. He looked over at her through the corner of his eye.

"Seth doesn't think it was an accident. He thinks someone was deliberately targeting the bus, and more to the point, you. That's what he went to talk to the deputies about. He also thinks we should be keeping an eye out for other attempts on you, that there will be more."

"Alex, that's ridiculous. Who would try to do something to me? Well, other than Seth."

"He didn't know. But he was fairly certain that he was right."

"And off we go!" The EMT—Judith—climbed back aboard. She was cheery and blond and in her early thirties. "We'll get you there quick as can be."

Angela and Alex passed the rest of the trip in silence, except for answering Judith's questions. Seth arrived at the hospital a little while later. When Deputy Rivera came over to ask her about the bus crash, she told the whole story as she knew it, and emphasized waking up to find Seth's hand under her bra. Deputy Rivera took her statement, and went to question Alex. Finally, she went to question Seth. Seth left the hospital in handcuffs.

CHAPTER

On Monday, Angela went to Ms. Lee's office with her mother as a phone call had instructed her to do. The office was painted a fairly drab tan color, but Ms. Lee had a tall plant in one corner and several paintings on the walls. The paintings were Chinese-style landscapes and pictures of river life. Seth and his mother were there as well. Seth's mother was dressed normally in a charcoal pants suit. Who knew where the goth came from?

Ms. Lee opened the meeting. "I'm sure you know why you're here. I am not prepared to tolerate assaults by one student on another. I understand the courts are still involved and have not yet rendered a decision, and also aware of Seth's claim of attempting to help. I must admit I find it somewhat difficult to believe, but Alex Menendez appears to think that Seth was trying to help." Her nostrils flared as she paused. "I am going to let the court decide any appropriate punishment. However, I also need to do something to keep the peace here at LVH. You don't share any classes. So, Seth, stay away from Angela. If you harass her or stay in her vicinity, I will suspend you. Is that understood?"

"I understand you. I never did her any harm. I was just trying to find a heart beat. But I do understand you and will comply," Seth replied to her. "Are we done here? I am not supposed to be this close to Ms. Fujimori." He didn't look like he'd be particularly obedient—and with that comment, didn't sound like it either. And he was lying about finding a heart beat. She knew that. She also sensed that accusing him of lying here wouldn't help anything, because she couldn't prove a thing. He would be staying away from her. Until the court handles him, that would have to do.

The day they were to play White Hill Christian dawned foggy. Angela was a back up today Coach Nguyen said. The doctors at Marin General had given her a clean bill of health and could find no reason she couldn't play. She may have been unconscious on the bus, but aside from the spot on the back of her head where she'd bled there was nothing wrong with her. 'Healthy as a horse" was the Kansas born doctor's pronouncement, no concussion or anything of the sort. It had frankly baffled Dr. Monaghan completely. He couldn't even figure out why she'd been knocked out, and there was no concussion. Nevertheless, Coach Nguyen decided to be careful with her.

Alex hadn't been quite as lucky. With all the cuts and bruises he'd suffered, he hadn't been give permission to suit up. Overall, he appeared fine. Better than the coach and the doctors thought he should be He'd come along, but he was holding a clipboard and acting as an assistant to Coach Nguyen. She saw his seven friends, though. Everyone except Seth. She had no idea where Seth might be, but she was relieved to know that he didn't seem to be there. Teddy Pope was there with the Lucas Valley High Christian Society. They usually met at the flagpole before school and prayed and listened to Teddy sermonize. She wasn't clear on how he'd gone from freshman recruit to leader of the group—she wasn't in it herself—but they were devoted to him. She'd heard several of them preface conversations with "Teddy says." Alex's other Friends were sitting together. She also saw her own friends—they'd brought a big "Go Angela!" sign. Carmen, Ruth, Anita, Liz, Marie, Shannon, Sara, Joy, and Karen were sitting together, as usual, but a few boys were sitting with them as well. And, surprisingly, the black crow figure of Seth. There had to be a fly.

As she looked up, a shadow passed over the field. A vulture soared overhead. A big vulture, with white under its wings. This far up in the hills, vultures weren't unusual, but the darkening of the sun was. Maybe it was an omen.

"Hey, Alex. Any idea what's up with the vulture? Maybe it's going to feast on White Hill players?"

Alex looked up. "Not a vulture. That is a good omen for the Thunderbolts. A thunder*bird*."

"Huh?" came from half a dozen players at once.

"That's a condor," he replied. "Ok, lads and lasses. Listen up they're playing Harry Simpson as their inside linebacker in place of John Davis. Harry's not very bright. Expect him to go straight for Tom every single play," he said, mentioning Tom Lewis, the senior quarterback.

"Their secondary is big, but slow. Ange can run rings around them, so help her out. If they can catch her, they can probably bring her down without much trouble. Same goes for Dan, Jimmy, and Atlee. Derek, Marvin" he said, addressing the two tight ends, "look to block. Tom should be able to get you the ball quite a bit.

"Jason, Bryan, Kevin, I hate to say it but their line is pretty good. You guys may be more effective protecting Tom than actually carrying the ball."

"And us?" asked Brent Smith, the left guard.

"Brent, you, Patrick, Michael, Jonathan, and Leo get the fun of taking on their line. Watch out particularly for their nose tackle, Billy Potter. My sources tell me he likes to play dirty."

"You got it, Alex. We'll bring this one in. What kind of a name is the Gideonites anyway?" Atoro Oshima wanted to know.

"Bolts on three!"

The offense chorused, "One, Two, Three—THUNDERBOLTS!"

The game seesawed back and forth. As expected, they played dirty. They seemed particularly interested in hitting Angela, or so it seemed to her. It was different players each time, but there were eight unnecessary roughness calls on the boys covering her. They were almost as bad with Dani; their first drive seemed to target her section of the field. Alex went over to encourage her, and she made them pay for targeting her. It suddenly seemed a lot easier for her to tackle. The receivers seemed to bump her a lot. There were five offensive pass interference calls on receivers in her sector—all on receivers hitting her, hard.

After checking on Dani, Alex went over to the sports drink coolers and looked at them closely. Then he poured himself a cup from each of them, stared at them, swished them around, and noticed Angela looking at him while the defense was on the field. He started sipping from them, pinky extended, and swishing the orange flavored sports drink—the company that had the county school contract to supply it to the sports teams kept reminding them that they weren't Gatorade, and their product shouldn't be referred to by someone else's brand name—around in his mouth like some snooty wine taster. When he came to one, though, he spat it out, and looked around. Then he 'accidentally' knocked it over the bench where it was and emptied it.

Ange could tell that he hadn't had an accident. He'd knocked the container over deliberately. When he got back from refilling it, he took a look at the other powder sports drink, and his face twisted. He checked the other coolers again, he then gathered up the powders, taking them over for inspection, she guessed. Then she had to go back on the field. They drove down the field and Angela caught one of Tom's passes. She never did figure out what Alex was up to with the drinks, and by the end of the game, she'd forgotten about it.

At the end of the game, Angela had two touchdown catches and Dani had a pick six. The White Hill Christian Gideonites had gone down 45 to 20, and they seemed very sullen about it. They said all the right things, the congratulations, but it didn't seem at all like they meant it. Angela thought she heard Seth congratulate her but he was still over by the bleachers talking to Alex when she thought she heard him, so it was just her imagination. The creepy goth still seemed to be staring at her quite a bit, even as she boarded the school bus to ride back down the hill to home and a soothing hot shower before heading over to Salerno's for pizza and afters.

Angela went home, showered, and changed before heading over to Salerno's. The pizza place served a thin crust pizza, but it was a soft thin crust. They also tossed the dough in the air as they made the pizza. A good portion of the team hadn't bothered doing much more than getting out of their pads, so when she got there the team had already gotten the party into swing. The team and the cheerleaders were sitting together, and Dani had obviously also taken advantage of the opportunity to go home first. The blond girl was wearing a 49ers jersey and white skirt, and talking avidly with some of the other backfield players. Angela went to the counter to order a pizza; Dad had handed her the money and told her to call when she was ready to come home. Since the place had expanded, there was also room for the Terra Linda High team. With the number of private schools in the county, the public ones celebrated their victories. Terra Linda had faced San Rafael, and had lost. They did come out to celebrate the defeat of White Hill Christian, though, and Erika O'Donnell was one of their back up quarterbacks.

"Hey, Angela. I heard you made their defense look foolish," Erika said to her as she took her table number and looked for a spot. Erika was a dark haired girl with hazel eyes.

"Well, I wouldn't go that far, but they've got big guys in the backfield."

"*I'd* go that far," Dani put in. "Your performance out there was nothing short of inspiring, chica." Dani had fallen in love with the word once she discovered it in Spanish. "Mine unfortunately…"

"I was watching, Dani. They were doing everything they could to hit you. Be careful of that, Erika. They seem to have a real problem with girls on the field. I expect you're going to be getting a lot of late hits," she advised the Terra Linda quarterback.

"Hey, thanks."

"Don't mention it. I'm sure Dani can get through your line to bring you down!" She grinned.

"Hey, thanks" she repeated in an all-together different tone.

"Don't mention it," she and Dani said in chorus. They grinned at each other. Angela and Dani found a table with Alex and Kevin Pastorini. They enjoyed the pizza and the pitchers of soda and the reminiscing on the game. She suddenly thought she heard Seth's voice saying "Be careful, Angela", but he was nowhere around.

"What's up, Ange?" Dani asked.

"Oh, nothing, I thought I heard something." That was twice today that she'd thought she'd heard Seth's voice.

"What did you hear?" Dani asked as she ate a slice of pepperoni and sausage.

"Oh, I thought I heard Creepazoid. Impossible, of course, since he's not here!"

"You heard Seth?" Alex asked, putting down his slice and wiping his fingers on a napkin. "What did he say?"

"Dude, what does it matter? She mistook something. Did that tree do something to your brain?" Kevin put in. Alex waved him to silence.

"I'd still like to know what she thought he was saying," Alex said.

"Oh, alright. I thought he said 'be careful', which doesn't make all that much sense."

Alex smiled. "No, no it doesn't. Excuse me, I need to hit the john." He got up and went back towards the men's room. The conversation at the table returned to football and school, and dropped the perve entirely.

Alex still wasn't back yet when a chime from her phone reminded Angela of her curfew. She called Dad and he said he'd be there soon. She decided to say her goodbyes and go out to wait for him.

She pulled out her phone to play a Tetris game, and was paying little attention to much of anything when she saw the dark blue Toyota pull up. Dad always got Toyotas. She moved towards the passenger side without paying much more attention; she was trying to get this block to fit. The door opened for her. "Ange! Wait! That's not your Dad!" Alex called from behind her. Huh? She looked up and Alex was right. But the two passengers got out surprisingly quickly; she must not have noticed them, and they grabbed her. Her foot lashed out, connecting with a knee, but they were still able to wrestle her into the car.

The driver reversed and started to drive off when it simply died and the tires went flat. Salerno's emptied as both teams surrounded the car and pounded on it. Seniors on the offensive line opened the driver's door and pulled him out, while the defensive linemen and linebackers pulled out the other two. "Angela? You okay?" came the call from outside the car.

"Yeah, I think so." Boys trying to tackle her had grabbed her more roughly in the game. She got out of the car. Same make and model as Dad's but if she'd been paying attention she would have noticed the different license plate. Dad had one with a whale's tail on it. This one was just a normal California plate. Why had that voice of warning been in Seth's voice?

The big boys from the line were sitting on the men who had tried to kidnap her. Erika came up to her, saying she'd already called the police. A squad car even beat Dad there, and the teams told their stories to the cops, who wrote everything down and took the three would-be kidnappers into custody. When Dad arrived, she'd already given her statement. With all the other witnesses, they let her go home.

Biology class was going to be a bear, Angela thought. She was sitting in the back with Carmen and Karen, and Bridget Sullivan up front was raising her hand at every question. She'd been doing it ever since school started, too. It was obvious from the complete answers she was giving that she was going to blow the curve into next year in this class. She didn't know Bridget well, but she was one of Alex's friends, and so was Malcolm Muir. Him she knew a bit better; he was on the local swim team with her friend Carmen Burns and class president Julian Kanekawa. Everyone was expecting Malcolm to join the school team. Malcolm wasn't raising his hand as often as Bridget was--in fact he often looked thoroughly bored--but whenever he was called on he sounded like he'd swallowed the textbook.

Mrs. Kravitz was a good teacher, though. She didn't always call on Bridget and Malcolm. By the end of class she'd stopped asking for volunteers and simply started calling on people. Unfortunately she started with Carmen and Carmen didn't know the answer. She called on Bridget next and got the answer she was looking for 1916.

Angela felt almost relieved to be in English Literature with Ms. Gonzalez. They were reading Shakespeare. Ms. Gonzalez had them reading his sonnets aloud in class, as well as composing their own. It was something of a drag, but at least it wasn't as bad as geometry. Her friends Karen MacLeod and Joanna Hughes were in this class. Karen was a cheerleader, and Joanna was going to be trying out for the volleyball team with her. She'd been surprised that Keisha Johnson was too. Keisha seemed to spend more time on her pad checking the stock market than she did paying attention to things like sports—or their English class--but her ability to return the next line of the sonnet or play was amazing.

Homework was a half a dozen sonnets to read and analyze by their next class. Keisha marked her with a friendly wave, but she had stuck with Karen and Joanna as study-buddies. They'd also partnered up in Spanish and History, so it made a lot of sense. They'd also gotten Dani to join in, so at least there was someone to talk football with. Alex was in a different section of the class, but he occasionally came by.

Fortunately Alex was back in practice; the cuts and abrasions he'd suffered in the bus crash were a lot more superficial than they'd appeared.

Today was tackling drills. Even the offense had to learn how to tackle, because there was always the chance of a fumble or an interception. So she got the joy of trying to bring down Dave Smith and Kevin Pastorini, a couple of juniors who played corner back. Both boys were quite a bit bigger than she was and they proved stronger, too.

"Ange, don't go for a body tackle, if you can help it. Aim for the legs. That's where we're vulnerable," Kevin said. "Let me show you. I can pick you up without much problem. Jump on my back and I can carry you with me. You might slow me down enough for someone else to make the tackle, but if you come in and get my legs, I trip and go down."

While Kevin was giving her tackling advice, she thought she saw people in all black sneaking in through a gap in the fence. "Kevin, what do you think they're up to?"

"Who, Ange?" he replied.

"Those people over there, by the fence gap," she said, pointing.

He looked. "I don't see anyone. What did that creep do to you, that you're seeing things?" He sounded angry.

"His hand down my bra."

"What a jerk. My dad's a lawyer, and said he's probably only going to get a few weekends in Juvie? That sucks, Ange. It really does." She couldn't quite put her finger on that note in his voice… or what he might be planning to do. But it sounded almost sweet to her. If only there wasn't that odd alarm bell going off in the back of her mind.

Angela slunk into the biology lab. The walls were covered in posters of cells and famous biologists—Rosalind Franklin, Jane Goodall, Dianne Fossey. Terrariums and fish tanks lined the walls, and she could see the fish weren't normal gold fish or even tropical fish. She looked around and saw that she was partnered with Bridget. Well, at least she was likely to pass Mrs. Kravitz' course, if that performance in class was anything to go on! Bridget had already gone beyond having the textbook memorized. She sat down next to Bridget and smiled at her. Bridget was wearing a T-shirt from the San Francisco Zoo, jeans, and had a flannel shirt around her waist. She wasn't wearing any jewelry or make up. There was a large backpack on the floor, a bag of candied bugs, and a green-fronted multi-subject notebook with recycled paper. "You must be Angela," she said.

"And you're Bridget. That was quite a performance yesterday." Bridget smiled back.

"Mom's a research biologist. She's always got the books and subscriptions lying around. If I don't get an "A" in here she'll be mighty disappointed in me. You're on the football team, right? Not just one of the cheering section?"

"Yeah. I'm a receiver. I've got a bunch of friends who tried out for cheerleading though."

"Fabulous! You're the one who caught the game winning touchdown, right?"

Angela smiled at her. The enthusiasm for the game was obvious in Bridget's tone. "Um, that was me, yeah."

"I won my bet with Dawn. Thanks!"

"What did you bet?" she asked, wondering how much it had been.

"Oh, just an exchange of services. She's going to help me with my project first, and then I'll help her with hers. It was really just about establishing which of us went first."

"Oh, okay. What's the answer to this lab of ours?"

"We're learning how to use these archaic microscopes, I think." The black and chrome microscopes, one to each pair of students, did look ancient. Glass slides were set in boxes between each pair. Mrs. Kravitz stood up in front of the class talking about how to prepare slides. Bridget took that moment to contemplate the salt-water aquarium on Mrs. Kravitz's left. Angela just sort of spaced out

"Mom taught me how to do this when I was little and we were in the Amazon. You should probably be paying a bit more attention," Bridget said to her sotto voce.

Whoops! She should have guessed someone like Bridget not paying attention meant that it was nothing new for her. She returned her attention to blond-from-a-bottle Mrs. Kravitz continuing to explain how to prepare a slide. She then called on Bridget. "Miss Sullivan! Since you're so interested in preparing slides, as is necessary in biology, perhaps you would care to demonstrate the proper procedure for doing so!"

Bridget smiled. "Of course, Mrs. Kravitz. I'd be happy to." She got up, went to the front of the class, selected a sample, prepared it, placed the small glass square delicately on top, and placed it under the microscope.

She looked through the lens, and adjusted it. Then she glanced at Ms. Kravitz, gave the dials another adjustment without looking through the lens, and gestured. "Did I do it correctly, Mrs. Kravitz?"

Mrs. Kravitz bent down and looked through the lens. She came back up and looked at Bridget, whose anxious face and hands clasped behind her back made her look the picture of innocence. "How did you do that?"

"I've been preparing slides since I was eight, ma'am." Mrs. Kravitz looked at her sternly for about thirty seconds before bursting out laughing.

"Ok, that's one on me! Thank you, Bridget. You may return to your seat. However, rather than you preparing the slides let's see how your lab partner does," she said.

"Oh, great," Angela said when Bridget resumed her seat.

"Oh, don't worry, it's not that hard. I'll talk you through it," Bridget replied. With her help, Angela finished well before the lab period was over. Mrs. Kravitz wouldn't let them go early—naturally—but she was generous enough to let them start looking over the next lab assignment.

"Isn't that thoughtful of her?"

"Prepare and diagram a plant cell," Bridget read. "Easy enough."

"For you, maybe! I can't get the hang of this, and I've got practice."

"Angela, there's nothing wrong with your mind. It's how you apply it. Football's fun, sure. But there are only so many spots open for girls to play professionally. Study your ass off and open up your options. I mean, whaddya wanna bet that Mrs. Kravitz NEVER calls on me again in lab thinking I don't know what I'm doing?"

"Well, when you put it that way..." Angela replied to her.

"Don't be *too* sure of that..." Mrs. Kravitz said quietly.

"I do. Study session fifth period? We can get the preparation done and look at the homework."

"OK. Where?"

"How about the library? It's got some private rooms for people so they won't be disturbed. And if you want, come over after school. Mom'll be fine with it"

That sounded a little more intense than Angela usually preferred to study, but all she said was "Okay". Maybe Bridget was on to something.

The locker rooms were attached to the gym, a big hard wood place where the basketball and volleyball teams played and the cheerleaders practiced. It was separated from the main school building by about a hundred feet. There were a couple of equipment rooms where students could check out a ball or something. The lines were purple, and "Go Thunderbolts!" was painted in a variety of places. Most of the internal walls were painted Thunderbolt yellow, and the corridor down to the girls' locker room was no exception. The girls' room was on one side of the building, the boys' room on the other. Almost—there was Chris Hayday, who seemed to plan on getting gender reassignment and used the girls' room. She was nice but shy, and seemed to realize that she made some of the other girls uncomfortable, so she usually came in early, changed, and left before the other girls were going to gym.

Angela had something of a premonition as she walked down to the girls' locker room that morning. She was late; the offense was supposed to do some early drills this morning but her parents had been slow getting going, and the refrigerator had suddenly and inexplicably died. It was as if everything had been conspiring against her that morning. It wasn't a chill, or a scent, it wasn't really anything that she could put into words, just the definite sense that something was horribly wrong. When she opened the door to the showers, she knew why.

Three girls lay dead. The heart of the cheerleader squad, Courtney Richardson, the head cheerleader, brown haired and blue eyed, had her throat slashed open and her heart ripped out. Her blood was spread all over the tiles. Tina Thompson was staked to the wall with long spikes, almost looking crucified, her blond hair coated in blood. Emma Rajani's sightless eyes stared at her headless corpse.

Angela stood there in horror for several minutes as her mind fought to take in the scene in front of her. Then she screamed and fled the room, her stomach rebelling at the sight she'd seen. She ran into Alex, knocking him down. "Wow, Ange, what's wrong?"

She gasped out, "Courtney... Emma... Tina... dead... murdered... in the showers..." she couldn't continue.

"Oh no, Ange," his arms went around her and squeezed. His sympathy and shared horror were obvious, and they helped to steady her, enough to take several deep breaths. "Can you get to the office? Get Ms. Lee? I'll stay out here and wait for people and keep them from going in, OK? Or do you want me to get her? You're a faster runner than I am."

"Yes, I can do that. I will do that. Thanks, Alex." She was relieved to have Alex calling the shots for this. His soothing command voice helped her settle her own mind. He was the quarterback in the huddle calling the play. Something ordinary to get her mind back in the game.

She ran for the office, and the principal, and the adults to take over. She knew the cheerleaders. This would devastate them. She was already thinking about how she would tell her friends and what she could do to help.

When she and Ms. Lee—who didn't move as fast in heels as Angela did in sneakers—got close, Angela could make out voices. "The killer was white, middle aged, brown hair, clean shaven, and male but no one that any of them recognized," Seth was saying. How could he possibly know that? And what was that about them recognizing the killer?

"Alex, I'm getting some residual power. There was a compulsion to this, but it wasn't on the girls, I'm positive," Teddy said. Huh? What was he talking about?

"That's what I was thinking," Alex replied.

"Seth, I'm thinking that they died between six and seven this morning, maybe around six-thirty. Does that match your impression?" That was Bridget, but... again, how would she know that? This was getting weird.

"Yes, but I need to get going. Ms. Lee brought Angela back with her," Seth replied. "I'll keep at it and let you know if there's any thing further to be extracted. Bridget, the clubhouse?" A few moments later Seth came walking past them. "Ms. Lee, Ms. Fujimori," he said as he passed them. Other than his little crystal headed flashlight glowing, nothing seemed odd about him. Then she stopped and stared at his retreating back. They hadn't been visible or talking. So how had he known she was coming back with the principal?

"Bridget, how did you know?" she asked once they'd arrived and Principal Lee had shunted them off, told them to go to class.

"My uncle's a medical examiner and has been giving me some training in that. It helps to know how long something you find in field research has been dead."

"Ah, ok, it was kind of weird that you knew that."

Bridget smiled. "Yeah, I suppose it was. If you want a tighter idea, ask Seth. He's even better at it than I am, which is why I asked him."

"Luckily, the creep's not supposed to be anywhere close to me."

"I've got his number if you want it. Since the cops are on the way, I've got Japanese this morning." Bridget looked back at her. "What were you doing here this early?"

"Oh, didn't Alex tell you? We were supposed to be running some drills."

"So the entire team knew?"

"No, just the offense."

"Ah. Okay. Later."

CHAPTER 4

Saint George's Episcopal Church was built in the fifties and it showed its age. It had a new coat of paint, but there were other places that needed repair or replacement. Angela and her parents had been coming here ever since they moved to the valley when Angela was seven. It was a warm and welcoming place, but over all small, and it wasn't in Lucas Valley proper. It was in the community of Terra Linda, a little south. Not that that made all that much difference; they could still get there fairly quickly.

Sunlight accompanied them to the church, the early sunlight of the day, when everything was fresh and new and unspoiled. And bright. Unfortunately bright, even with her nice dark glasses on. The glasses would help disguise her if she fell back asleep during the sermon. She sat in the back, phone out and engaged in a game app. It was chilly enough out that Dad didn't have the window rolled down, the way he liked to do. Which also meant her hair wouldn't be mussed by Dad's open window.

Mom and Dad had flipped a coin to see who would drive. Mom won, so she was driving. They picked Granma up from Water Lilies, and sang early morning wake up songs, notably "Don't Worry, Be Happy". It was hard to be so cheery so early in the morning. They found parking—there were plenty of spaces. Catching the early early service so as to not run into the televised football games starting at ten made sense to Angela and Dad, not so much to Mom. Mom was a fan, too; she just thought church should have priority over football. At least if the Raiders didn't have an early game. Once they got back home, Mom would make a run to Kaiser's Hof Brau for sandwiches. Dad had always said their pastrami was the best food this side of the Pacific. Angela didn't quite know about THAT, but they were really good. None of that thin-sliced stuff you got in a deli. She almost wished she were going with Mom to watch the carvers do their stuff on the meats.

The early early service was always lightly attended, and today was no exception. Mostly other football fanatic families who didn't want to miss church, either—or at least had someone to insist on not missing. Mother Elaine was a morning person, and a lively one at that. More than one person at the early early service grumbled at her cheerfulness from the pulpit. Her graying black hair and bright blue eyes were a welcome sight at any time, especially when you were still half asleep and in your Sunday best… although a lot of people seemed to be wearing 49er and Raiders jerseys instead. Mom would never let her get away with that. God knew she'd tried.

"Good morning, happy parishioners! It's good to see so many people here this early, and Go Niners!" That got a chuckle. "And God bless the Raiders, they need it." That got another one. "God grant that no one be injured and may the best teams win today." From there she launched into the usual preliminaries and sermon. Angela was attentive to the service— well as attentive as anyone here this early. The sermon focused on matters of forgiveness of those who had wronged you accidentally.

After communion, Angela thanked Mother Elaine, and chatted with some of the others there that morning. She was talking with a boy— Michael Curley-- who went to Terra Linda High when a small plane came hurtling out of the sky, straight at her. She could see the pilot, struggling mightily with the controls of the plane to no effect, and she couldn't move she couldn't get her legs to do anything. She just stood there paralyzed when a powerful gust of wind caught the plane's wings and lifted it, its fixed wheels passing inches over her head, to crash into the church. Mother Elaine screamed for helpers as Mom and Dad rushed over to her, shouting at her to find out if she was alright, if the plane had come as near as it looked to hitting her.

"Thank God you're okay, Angela. Mike, are you hurt? No? Thank God," Mother Elaine said. "Can we get the poor pilot out?" She ran around organizing things, and people leaped forward to help. There was, remarkably no movie-style explosion from where the plane had impacted the church. Mother Elaine had the teenagers present corral the younger kids and keep them out of the church while the adults went back in. Dad and Mr. Singh pulled the pilot out, and after that they waited for the fire department, since the wings of the plane were leaking fuel.

"I don't know what happened," the pilot said. "One minute everything was fine, I was on my way to Half Moon Bay, and then it was like something else had control of the plane. I couldn't get it to respond at all." He had a number of scratches on him, but otherwise seemed in remarkably good shape. Dr. Helen Gotanda was keeping him from getting up and moving around, insisting that he wait for the paramedics. Moving him out of a building that might collapse or catch on fire was all she was willing to permit.

Angela looked back towards the church. The stained glass was gone, shattered by the nose of the plane. Pieces of the plane and the church were scattered all over the lawn, some out into the parking lot. The benches and walkways in the grounds were mostly clear, but it would be some time before the church could be used again. A number of people from the nearby Catholic church rushed over, asking if people were okay.

She saw one of the priests from the Catholic church talking to Mother Elaine and the two junior Episcopalian priests. Father Michael gave boring sermons. Father Dominic wasn't as boring—he was as with it as he could be—but he wasn't as fun as Mother Elaine, either. Mother Elaine held up her hands. "Everyone! Father Jarod has invited us to hold services next door at Saint Teresa's while we repair Saint George's. Let's give our brothers and sisters a mighty thank you!" There was a loud "Hurrah!" and Mother Elaine continued. "And I seem to have left my tablet on the lectern. Could I borrow someone's to put that out on our website?" There was a bit of a ripple of laughter around the congregation as several were offered up. Mother Elaine borrowed the first one she got to.

The ambulances and fire trucks arrived, and the police shortly thereafter. They answered the questions from the police, and were told that the FAA would probably be contacting them. The pilot was taken to the hospital. With nothing left to do, they got in their cars and went home.

Angela was the only one who noticed the figure on the hill overlooking the church. And since no one else noticed the figure at all, no one noticed it do the impossible and vanish into thin air when Angela's back was turned.

The county civic center—which included the courtrooms--was certainly an odd building. Stretching between two hilltops, the roof was blue, and everything was circles and semicircles, none of the Greek or Roman columns and steps you saw on TV. The walls were pink tinged tan, and brass railings were common. There was a short tunnel at the saddle of the hills where cars could drive through and let people off. The building had a peculiar odor all it's own, so odd that she could never quite describe it.

They couldn't use the tunnel. Dad was coming with her, and they weren't actually going to court today. They were going to talk to the assistant district attorney assigned to the case of Seth Dupree, Marguerite Zuccaro. It took them a couple of minutes to walk down the corridors… open to the planters below—and reach the DA's office. Dad introduced them and they sat down. The young man at the desk called Ms. Zuccaro's number and said it would be just a few minutes. Of course. She pulled out her tablet and got to work on some geometry homework. Dad pulled out a newspaper; as he flipped the pages she saw a story about a bunch of wild boar being found dead. She didn't know why it caught her eye; it wasn't like she was a boar hunter.

They sat there fore a while as people came and went, and then Ms. Zuccaro opened the inner door. "Mr. Fujimori? Ms. Fujimori? I'm Marguerite Zuccaro. Please, come with me." Ms. Zuccaro was tall, black haired with a prominent nose and couldn't be out of her twenties yet. She wore a white blouse and gray suit with a minimum of jewelry—stud earrings, a pendant less chain necklace—or make up, just lipstick. They followed her back to a small office. Ms. Zuccaro picked stacks of binders off the two visitor chairs. "Please, sit."

Angela and Dad sat in the indicated chairs. "Is there a court date yet, Ms. Zuccaro?" Dad asked.

"That's one of the things I wanted to talk to you about. Mr. Dupree has offered to plead no contest to simple battery and accept a sentence of five weekends in juvenile hall with a certain amount of community service—we're still working on just how much-- and not be permitted within fifty feet of you outside school for a year, and only incidental contact even there. He wouldn't be taking the bus with you any more, either. What do you think?"

"That's it?" Dad said.

"We have a proof problem here, Mr. Fujimori. There's an intent element for a sexual assault charge that we've got a real problem proving. We can't prove why he decided to put his hand where he did, but he's claiming he was trying to find a heartbeat. That puts it into the realm of trying to administer first aid to an unconscious person, for which consent is legally presumed. It's not the normal method—that would be checking for a pulse on the neck or wrist—but Mr. Dupree has never taken a first aid class, so there's the possibility that he doesn't know that. Mr. Menendez says he wasn't watching, that he was hurting and dealing with his own injuries at the time and can't say one way or the other what Mr. Dupree was doing. He did say he told Mr. Dupree to check on your daughter before helping him. He simply wasn't paying attention, according to him. Mr. Menendez further strikes me as a poor witness against Mr. Dupree. They've been friends since preschool. He can't—or won't—do anything more than confirm what Mr. Dupree is already admitting he did. In fact, we've gotten more from Mr. Dupree than we have from Mr. Menendez. Mr. Menendez also says that Mr. Dupree and your daughter don't particularly like each other and never have, but that Mr. Dupree is a helpful person and accepted the instruction to check your daughter out without question."

"But... he was copping a feel! I thought that was…"Angela protested.

"I think so too, Ms. Fujimori. Unfortunately, what you know and I know and what a jury will probably think was happening isn't the same as being able to prove what was happening and why it was happening. Mr. Menendez wasn't paying attention. You were unconscious. Ms. Stoddard is dead. The only person alive, awake, and aware of what was happening is Mr. Dupree."

"Ok, I can see that. What do you think of his offer?" Dad said.

"Honestly? I think there's a good chance he could walk under the circumstances. The possibility that he really was trying to help, especially with Mr. Menendez's testimony about what he told Mr. Dupree to do, means we could lose."

Angela's eyes wandered over the books and binders on the shelves. The idea that Seth would escape all punishment was almost as bad as the thought of him touching her. They let her sit there for several minutes. "Can you get him more time in Juvie?" she finally said.

"Unfortunately, probably not." She started raising fingers with her points. "He's only fourteen. He has no record. He appears to be contrite. It was only a touch; his victim suffered a violation but no damage." She returned her hand to the desk. "He's already offering more time than I think he'd normally get. A fine and community service would normally be it, I'm afraid. If we win, which as I said, is not guaranteed."

Angela and her father sat in the courtroom next to Ms. Lee, the principal. Seth was at a table next to his own father and a middle-aged, dark haired woman in a dark gray suit, his attorney. Ms. Zuccaro sat at the other table. As it was a juvenile hearing, the only other people present were the bailiff—a tough looking man with dark skin and Latino features--and a clerk, a young Asian man. The room was paneled in light wood, the great seal of California behind the judge, and the flags flanking the judge's seat.

"All rise," the clerk said. "Juvenile Court is now in session. The Honorable Mary Shaefer Judge presiding."

"Be seated," said the gray haired judge. She looked to be in her sixties. "Ms. Zuccaro, I understand we have an agreement?"

"Yes, Your Honor. A no contest plea to simple battery. Five weekends in Juvenile Hall, two hundred hours of community service at one of the accepted facilities. And outside of school he's not to be permitted within fifty feet of Ms. Angela Fujimori for a year."

The judge considered it for a few minutes.

"Mr. Dupree, please rise and inform the court as to what happened."

Seth stood up. "Yes, Your Honor. The bus hit something, I don't know what, and went through a bunch of trees into the creek. Branches came in through the windows and cut up Alex. Alexander Menendez. Angela was bounced up out of her seat and hit her head on one of the seat backs, I think. I grabbed the seat back and managed to stay put. I heard Ms. Edie scream. When we stopped I checked on Alex and he said he'd be fine, to check on Angela. I was the only person not hurt. I got Angela on to the floor and checked for a pulse. I didn't find one, so I kept one hand—my left-- on her forehead and reached with my right hand under her clothes to see if her heart was beating, and my fingers touched her breast. I'm sorry it happened and even sorrier that I touched her inappropriately."

Angela sat back, stunned. Seth had just lied, she was sure of it. About looking for a heartbeat. About being sorry—he didn't regret it at all. Even about grabbing the seat back and staying put! She couldn't say why she was so absolutely certain, just as she couldn't seem to open her mouth and call him on it. The judge listened impassively.

"Well, Mr. Dupree, I accept the agreement reached by your counsel and the District Attorney. You'll start serving time this weekend."

"Yes, Your Honor," Seth replied.

Angela and Dad were walking down to their car—they'd visited the library after court—and saw Seth and his father on the way out. They also saw sheriff's deputies bringing in a medium height brown haired man in his forties, who was ranting something. "What's his problem?"

"That's the guy who murdered the cheerleaders a couple weeks ago," Seth said. She hadn't realized he could hear her. "You were supposed to be there early that morning, weren't you?"

"Yes, I was. What's your point?"

"I'm glad you weren't there." He dipped his head to her and went off a different way in the parking lot. She and Dad stared after him. What was with him?

CHAPTER

Angela wiped sweat from her brow as she stood in the line after Alex. Keisha Johnson had set up a lemonade stand, of all things, when practices got so popular. The stand itself was painted LVHS purple and yellow, made of plywood, and designed to be folded up and put in a car at the end of practice. She'd extend credit to the players, too… up to ten bucks, and then they were cut off until they cleared the tab. Spectators had to pay up front. Fortunately Seth hadn't been at a practice ever since that bus ride. She still thought he was watching somehow. Keisha bustled about, her Afro tall and proud, her red t-shirt emblazoned with the 49ers logo, her black jeans a new designer, her shoes teal. Mike Wu, a sophomore and running back, was in line before them.

"Mind if I ask you something, Keisha?" he asked

"Fire away, Mike," she replied

"You interested in going to the homecoming dance with me this weekend?" That elicited grunts of surprise from most people standing around near enough to hear.

Keisha looked at him, blinking several times. "Sure, Mike. Let me handle the customers, and we can talk later."

"Sure, I'll give you a hand with tear-down." Keisha's eyebrows and lips both twitched at Mike's comment for some reason.

"Well, tear it down fold it up and put it in my purse, but that'd be good." Mike smiled, nodded and took his lemonade. He didn't seem to turn a hair at her odd phrase.

"Hey, Keisha. You and Mike, huh? Not a pairing I was expecting. Does he know?"

"No more than Dani does, unless you told her something last time she sacked you in practice," Keisha replied. "What's your pleasure?"

"Real lemonade." Keisha offered real lemonade or powdered. "How'd the project go?" Alex asked.

"I think we got everything nailed down, or at least who wants where. You wanted Oakland, right? No one else did."

"Berkeley, yeah, who am I facing across the bay?"

"Malcolm's in the City, and I took San Jose."

"Bridget's up in Arcata, right?"

"Yuppers. Teddy's in Fresno, Jenny's in San Diego, Solly's in Sacramento, Dawn's in Hollywood, and Seth's in Santa Cruz."

"He's leaving for Santa Cruz?" Angela interjected. She'd calculated, and this would be Seth's first weekend free since he was sentenced. "COOL! Means skipping the boardwalk but…" Keisha and Alex were looking at her.

"Um, not quite, Ange. Not for about four years. This is something else," Alex replied.

"Yeah, we're starting a football league," Keisha said.

"Keisha, isn't that supposed to be under wraps?" Alex asked.

"Who's going to believe it's us, Alex? We can shout it from rooftops and put it all over the net, and no one's going to believe nine fourteen year olds are in charge of the league."

"Well, remind me to root against Santa Cruz."

"What name did he go with, anyway?"

"It's Seth. Take a guess."

"Right. Valkyries."

"Valkyries? Um, why is that name familiar?"

"There's an Operation Valkyrie movie about assassinating Adolf Hitler." Alex replied.

"According to Norse mythology, valkyries are beautiful warrior women, riding the offspring of Sleipnir, who choose heroes fallen in battle to join the ranks of the Aesir come Ragnarok," Keisha replied. "Sort of angels of heroic death."

"And that's a name for a football team?" Angela asked.

"Well, the GSFL is a professional women's league. We've already got the funding and the advertising and we settle the seven year contracts to distribute next week."

"So what's your team, Alex?"

"The Berkeley Avengers. Purple and Gold."

"Kind of like US, you mean?"

"Yeah, well… What are your colors, Keisha?"

"The San Jose Sphinxes will be in orange and bronze, thank you very much." At Angela's quizzical expression, she said, "Egyptian sphinxes tend to be male, yes, but the Greek Sphinx was female."

"Ah, OK. What are the other names? Do you know?" she asked.

"Sure I do," Keisha replied. "The Unicorns, the Furies, the Starlets, the Amazons, the Witches, and the Sirens." With raised eyebrows she looked at Alex. "Care to guess who's who? And what will you have Angela?"

"Real lemonade," she replied as Alex answered Keisha.

"Unicorns are easy—that's got to be Bridget. Witches would be Jennifer. Furies… the alliteration makes me think Teddy. Starlets… only place that makes sense is Hollywood, which means Dawn. I'm going to guess Malcolm's got the Sirens, which leaves Solomon with the Amazons. How'd I do?"

"Perfect. Now, we've taken long enough chatting, so if you could please move along? Yes, Johnny, what would you like?"

Angela and Alex walked away from the stand, Angela mulling over the conversation between Alex and Keisha. "Alex, how did you fund this?"

"Keisha's got ways, mysterious ways… that all have to do with commodities. She took a small stake from us—our college savings—and made it grow. She made us a killing." He looked at her. "Keisha's dad's a broker, her mother an investment banker. She comes by her witchy money making skills honestly, if that's what you're wondering. It's not like we robbed a bank or sold drugs…well, that part may not be true. I think she cornered a market in flu vaccine last year." He smiled. "If you really want the gory details and don't think they'd put you to sleep, ask her about it sometime."

"Maybe I will."

Homework. Blech. Angela had a TV feed on her laptop going, while she worked on her geometry. Mom and Dad didn't like it when she did that, but in this case it was the local news. That was okay, since "you need to know what's going on in the world, sweetie!" And it wasn't that distracting. It was, after all, the news.

"And officials at Marin Juvenile Hall are at a loss to explain how three different gangs in the hall came down with plague over the weekend, each gang getting a different variety of plague. No one else at the detention facility seems to have contracted the highly contagious disease, and they've all been given clean bills of health. According to one source, the gangs have virtually nothing in common, and are in fact usually opposed to each other, so how the Yersina pestis was transmitted is unclear. The inmates are being decontaminated and the entire facility fumigated to kill any fleas."

She grabbed her phone and hit Alex's number. Had she sent Seth to die?

"Hi Angela! What's up?"

"I just saw this story on the news, Alex. About plague in Juvie. I don't like him, but is Seth okay? I wanted him punished, not dead."

"Oh, no need to worry on that score. He's fine. Black Death won't touch him. He's made himself immune to it. And according to him it was fairly mild. It might not be next time they decide he's an easy target, though."

"Huh? What do you mean?"

"Never mind. Have you done the Spanish yet?"

"No, I'm still on geometry. And I think I hear Mom coming, so see you tomorrow!"

"See you tomorrow." That had been weird. It almost sounded as if Seth was the source of the plague, but that couldn't be true. Alex had just been pulling her leg.

"Sweetie, who were you talking to?"

She debated lying, and decided not to. "Alex. There was a news story about a disease outbreak at Juvie. I wanted to know if his friend had caught it."

"That was kind of you, dear, but get your homework done. Hand me your phone, you can have it back tomorrow." Mom had a thing about interrupting homework to take a phone call. She sighed and handed over the phone. Back to homework…

Angela was relieved that math was over, although Keisha stayed behind to talk to Ms. Winter. Geometry wasn't her best subject, and Room 134 wasn't exactly reassuring with the quotes and equations on the walls. Ms. Winter was a perfectly nice teacher, but she had enough quirks and aphorisms that made Angela wish she was allowed to bring in a translation computer. She grabbed her pack and her book, stuffed them in her pack, and strode out the door. She had to get to English three hallways over, and nearly ran into Seth waiting calmly in the hall with Teddy Pope. She'd gotten used to Seth waiting for the classroom. Teddy unfortunately, was in fine, full, and annoying voice.

"Ah, the prodigal girlfriend returns! Such love as she has for you…" She felt a sudden warmth of feeling for Seth.

"Knock it off, Teddy." Seth's voice was cool and distant as he averted his eyes from her and stared out the window into the oleander. The feeling of warmth vanished, although she was glad that Seth seemed to be taking her side. Angela ignored him to glare at Teddy.

"Ah, but she does! You can see it in her eyes!"

"I do not love him you ass. I want nothing to do with him. He's just a dreamy…." Teddy smiled slightly as she trailed off. She really could start seeing an attractive quality to Seth.

"Knock it off, Teddy." She shook her head and it vanished. She got the impression that Seth was smirking. A number of people in the hall were looking at Teddy with rapt attention, eyes almost glossing over as the gazed at and listened to Teddy.

"Ah, but all can see that you did give your heart to him, that it started truly beating only at his touch…" Once more the notion of Seth as her boyfriend, the one true love of her life rose in her mind with a magical feel, that he was the prince on a pale palomino steed come to…

"Knock. It. Off. Teddy." His actual cracking voice once more penetrated the weird haze. Color rose in her cheeks as she realized what she'd been feeling and just how ridiculous it was.

Teddy, however, returned to the attack. Every word he spoke was dripping with honey and she started believing when he began praising her and Seth as the most romantic couple since Romeo and Juliet... "You know, that was two people our age engaging in a murder-suicide pact." With a single sentence Seth brought the classic tale crashing down, her eyes blinking rapidly as something dark passed over the sun, and with it any particular desire to remain in his presence a moment longer. She turned and ran, almost fled, down the corridor to English. Studying Shakespeare would be a lot better than staying here. Out of the corner of her eye she saw Seth grab Teddy by the shirt and pull him into the classroom. As she left, she heard him say to Teddy, "Really? Mind games? With me standing right here?"

Even as she walked away, she saw a number of other people seemingly blinking almost as furiously as she was. What had come over her, thinking Seth might be cute? Thank god she stopped whenever he opened his mouth!

The Homecoming Dance. Balloons cavorted on the ceiling of the gym and streamers hung down, the giant banner over the stage. Angela arrived in a red gown on Robert Hammond's arm, and the strong safety spotted Alex and Dani. They headed over towards their teammates. Alex was wearing one of his father's gray suits and a yellow tie—the suit was still too large for him—while Dani was in a tight black dress, a little long for her. Robert's borrowed brown suit fit him much better. They smiled and talked football; they had just beaten Mount Tam High and were looking forward to playing Reagan High next week.

"Alex! Dani! Angela! Rob" Keisha and Mike walked up to them, Keisha in a glittering gold gown that seemed to fit her perfectly. They talked more football... and teachers, with Rob and Mike recommending against some and for others to the freshmen, She noticed as other people started to arrive. Some of them waived to Alex, like Teddy Pope, whose date looked like she'd stepped out of a Victorian Christmas card, or Solomon Levison, who was wearing an actual tuxedo and had brought Samiha Ali. Bridget had come with Julian Kanekawa. Dani was swept away with some of her friends and Mike and Rob went to get drinks. Bridget got up and came over to their little group, noticing Angela looking around nervously.

"He's not coming, you know," Bridget said, looking amused.

"Who?" she asked

"Seth. He's in Juvie still. No one's trying to bully him in there anymore, of course, but he's still stuck there one more weekend," she responded.

"What do you mean, no one's trying to bully him?"

Bridget smiled. "Don't worry about it, Ange. That's a beautiful dress, by the way. Where'd you get it?"

"Oh, have you been to Janice's, over in Northgate? They have a wonderful selection."

"Not yet, but maybe for next time."

Angela was returning to the gym from the girls' room when she over heard voices in the office. It was Teddy Pope most prominently, but the conversation was strange to say the least.

"She's been brainwashed and dominated completely. To quote Mr. Bryan, it's like pulling teeth to get her to give an actual opinion of her own. I think our problem is up that hill."

"And just how is that different from your groupies, Teddy?" a girl asked. "It's not like we don't hear them parroting you more than expressing their own opinions."

"I hear your concerns, Jenny. I'm not actually dominating anyone. I think that the people that are still in that group are people who are prone to cults and control. They're almost eager to let someone who "speaks for God" tell them what to do, what to think, and how to be. If it's not me, it *will* be someone else. I'm not actually exerting myself with them. They can exercise their own minds and wills whenever they wish to do so. Someone might have to teach them *how*, though.

"By contrast, Sarah Campbell actually has a fairly capable mind. It's been ground down with religious nonsense about what's "appropriate" for a girl and constantly reinforced… I'd call it abuse… but anyway, there's a control there that's definitely external. Ordinarily, we'd expect her to reassert control of herself shortly after whoever is providing the external control got distracted or chose to do something else. She's not doing that."

"Can we do something about it?" Alex asked.

"We can, but the reason I'm bringing this to everyone…well, everyone but Seth. What possessed him to agree to that, anyway?" Teddy sounded quite irritated.

"Never mind, Teddy. We really shouldn't be gone that long from the dance," said another girl. "And, if as you say Sarah's compromised, you shouldn't be away from her very long."

"Right, right. Well, someone pass this on to Seth?"

"I will. He and I are out at Fort Cronkite Monday afternoon for the Venusian project," the second girl responded.

"Good luck with that. Anyway, there's a solid chance that if I act to eliminate the external control, the girl will be seriously, maybe permanently damaged. I think the risk is worth it to find out who is controlling her, but you've made your positions clear. This is something to be decided by all of us, or I'd have already acted."

A figure sneaking—that was the only way to describe how she was moving—towards the locker room caught her eye. She was torn between continuing to listen to this bizarre conversation and figuring out what whoever was sneaking into the locker room was up to. Whatever the conversation was about, though, she could ask Alex or Bridget later. She slipped out of her shoes and padded quietly after the sneak. She hadn't gotten a good look, but none of the guys were wearing ball gowns. True, some were in kilts, though she supposed it could be Seth violating the terms of his plea bargain.

She got down stairs carefully. Her eyesight seemed better in the dark than usual, seeing well despite the shadows and absence of light. For some reason the intruder had gone into the boys' locker room. She put a hand to the door, hesitated, then shrugged and opened it. The boys wouldn't be in there now, at any rate. The girl had opened a locker and was pawing through it. Angela hit the lights.

It was Teddy Pope's nameless date. "Hey!" Angela grabbed a football that had been left lying around and threw it at her. Then she tackled the girl—Coach Nguyen's tackling drills came in handy. She hit the girl center of mass with her shoulder, slamming her into the lockers. Unfortunately, in football, once you'd tackled someone the play was over and you were supposed to release them.

The girl was stunned a bit by being slammed into the lockers, but she recovered and brought both her fists down on Angela's back, knocking her away, and tried to escape. Angela caught her by the ankle and pulled. The girl fell into a bench, then kicked out with her other foot and the toe caught Angela in the face, making her release the girl. She got up and ran for the door. Angela grabbed up a baseball and threw it, hard at the girl's fleeing back. She cried out in pain then paused, and turned back. "I had not known who I faced, whore." She leaped on Angela and started punching her in the face and head before Angela twisted and threw her off into a pile of equipment by the door. She found a baseball bat one of the boys had left in a stand by the door. With a shriek she swung it at Angela's head. Angela ducked and threw a football at the girl's chest, hitting it dead center and knocking the wind out of her. Angela then grabbed the girl's arms—training with the football team was proving useful in all sorts of ways—and pinned them behind her. The girl suddenly stopped fighting her and began weeping. She forced the girl to march forward, towards the room where Teddy had been talking. On arrival, there were eight people leaving.

"I followed this bitch into the boys' locker room, and she was stealing something out of one of the lockers. Since she's yours, I figured I'd return her to you," she said to Teddy.

He nodded soberly at her. "Thank you, Angela. Do you choose to involve the police, or do you wish me to deal with this matter? Either way is fine with me." He seemed completely sincere.

The last time she dealt with the police the boy who touched her has gotten off very lightly. She didn't really trust them not to be more trouble for her than it was worth. They might even decide to charge her with attacking the thief! "You deal with it," she said.

"Fair enough. Sarah, come with me. We're leaving, since you can't behave like a lady," Teddy said commandingly to the girl. She bowed her head and followed him. Angela started to join Alex and the others and go back to the party, but Bridget and this other red head—well there were three redheads n the group, but Dawn Takugawa was rather striking in her features—grabbed her and marched her towards the girl's bathroom. "You are NOT going back in there until we've fixed your face and your dress, Angela!"

"Oh," she said, slightly embarrassed. She'd just been fighting, so naturally it was smudged.

"I'm Jennifer, by the way. Bridget's been so enthusiastic about you that I've been meaning to meet you. Great game the other day," the other redhead said as she pulled a sewing kit out of her purse. "Never know when you'll need one of these. They're really handy to have. I don't suppose you sew?"

"Ah, not very well. I mean, I know the basics, but it'll take me a few hours to get this fixed." The worst part was she didn't remember the dress ripping in the fight.

"Well, in that case, just stand still, okay? I'll have it fixed in two shakes of a lamb's tail, as my great grandmother says." She rolled her eyes at the weird expression. "She's from Kansas. Doesn't have too much time left, I'm afraid."

"Hold still for me, too, Angela," Bridget said, grabbing her jaw. It'll be easier if I fix your make-up. And pay no attention to our muttering, We often do that when we're doing this. Sometime I'll have to tell you about the last time Keisha didn't have the hem high enough and went out in the rain! She was lucky we were around. Let's see, do I have that shade? No, it's not what I'm wearing so I don't. But what's this? Oh, I wore this to that thing over the summer, let's see... it doesn't match but it DOES go very nicely with what we can salvage. You'll look exotic rather than ruined. You okay with 'exotic'? Like something off the red carpet?"

"Really? Sounds fabulous!" she and the other two girls shared a grin as she stole Bridget's word.

"Groovy," Jennifer put in. She and Bridget chuckled at her expression. "Mom and Dad made it big in catering to counterculture and such, but they connect with it personally. Now, just a few more stitches... there we go! All set at this end, Bridget. How's the make-up coming?"

"Just a little bit more, a few finishing touches, and voila! How's she look, Jenny?"

"Groovy. She'll knock his socks off, whoever he is, or is it she? Take yourself a look in the mirror and tell us if you like it."

"He, he's definitely a he," Angela said as she looked herself over in the mirror. They certainly were fast. But everything appeared good, including the dress. It wasn't even a "get this pinned up" job there; the stitching may have been quick but it looked solid. And now it was time to get back to the dance. She'd be bruised tomorrow, but she felt great tonight.

The next Friday night they played out in the southern part of the county, against Reagan High. It was another private school, and was small enough that it was barely able to put a team together. Half a dozen girls played on the team just to round it out. If just a few players got seriously injured they'd have to forfeit the game or go "iron man" style and play defenders on offense or vice-versa.

Keisha Johnson, she of the lemonade stands at practice, had volunteered to take over running the sports drinks and water. Alex had talked her into it apparently. Mike Wu and some of the other guys had given her a hand setting up.

They won the toss and took the ball first. Angela was the receiver to run the ball back, and she caught it at the 20-yard line. The Gippers' kicking team was coming straight at her and she charged forward, getting around one then another, receiving blocks from her teammates, and then hit her stride down the sideline. She sped up under the lights and dodged around their kicker, going, going... she crossed the goal line and she'd made it! Touchdown!

"Good run, Angela. Knew you had it in you. Sit down for a bit," Coach Nguyen said.

"Thanks, Coach. Coach, something's been bothering me all week."

"What is it, Ange?" He asked, a little distracted as he sent his own kicking squad out onto the field.'

"What's a gipper?" They grinned at each other.

The Gippers' kick returner was stopped at the thirty-five, and the defense went to work. They did okay, and made the Gippers settle for a field goal. The coach held Ange out on the next series, and the Gippers' defense managed to stop them. Then they got stopped. Just before half time, with the score seventeen to ten, Coach Nguyen sent Angela back in. Angela caught several passes as they marched down the field, but this time Tom was intercepted and the Reagan player managed to run it back for a touchdown. On the same play, Tom was hit hard.

As they went into the locker room, she heard Alex thank Keisha for keeping everything safe. Safe? The sports drink? "Hey Alex, what's unsafe about the sportsade?" she asked him as they went in.

"Nothing, fortunately," he replied. "I think they did something to the water up at White Hill."

"Like what?"

"I dunno, but it smelled terrible."

"Ah, gotcha." It certainly explained Alex's actions.

When they came back out, Alex got the start in the second half, and that made a massive difference. Everyone was moving as part of the team, and unlike Tom, Alex would call an audible that worked. In fact, the audibles seemed to work better than the plays the coach sent in. Alex marched them right down the field and tossed a pass to Angela for the touchdown.

The Gippers had a problem on offense; Dani got through and sacked their quarterback. They soon had to punt, and Alex marched the Thunderbolts down the field again, and once more the touchdown pass went to Angela. They were up fourteen points when one of the Gippers injured Dani.

It didn't look like he meant to, they were both going for the ball when his foot connected with her ankle. Angela went over to see how she was. Oddly enough, Alex paused to exchange a look with Keisha before he went to check up on her.

Despite the distraction of Dani going down, Alex kept focused on the next couple of drives. He and Angela connected again for a fourth touchdown, and he ran it in himself for another one. With Alex as the quarterback, their defense wasn't doing anywhere near as well. All the same, Dani going down disheartened their own defense, and it was only by seven points that they ended up winning.

Alex was late getting into the locker room to change; Angela had already finished, helped Dani, and been seated outside when Alex walked in with a fairly grim look on his face. He smiled at the girls but he didn't stop to chat. He just went in. Once Alex was out of uniform and in sweats, the girls came in for the after game speech.

Angela rode home with Bridget after school. She didn't have practice today, and Bridget wanted to study for the big bio test on Thursday. She did decline the scorpion lollipops, though. The bus took them the opposite way from how to get to her house. Her eyes bugged out as they walked up the path. The house was enormous. The grounds were carefully landscaped, but there was something about the plants… "California… and more to the point, MARIN… native species, all of them. Mom's touch." The trees were redwood and manzanita and oak. Small lizards abounded, and the flowering shrubs were attracting butterflies more than bees.

"I never knew biology paid this well!" Bridget giggled at the comment.

"It doesn't. The money in the family comes from Dad," she replied. "He's in North Dakota this week, so Mom and I have the place to ourselves."

"What's he do?" she asked. Whatever it was obviously paid very well for a place like this. It was well out towards the coast. Bridget's home was round towers and large doors, built of redwood and three stories tall. Few places in the valley were two stories tall, and this place nestled in amongst the redwoods beautifully. She could almost see the deer coming in as welcome guests rather than the vermin devourers of gardens most seemed to think of them as. As they approached she could see the paddock and stable in the back.

"Have you heard of the Wildlife?"

"The casinos? Reno, South Lake Tahoe, Las Vegas? Yeah, I've seen them on ski trips. We even tried the buffet at Tahoe."

"That's it," Bridget confirmed, nodding.

"He's an executive or something?"

"No, he's the owner. He and Mom have a lot of interests in common, he's just not as good at field research, or lab work. So he took his inheritance and transformed it into the Wildlife. He's in North Dakota sorting out a supply problem with the bison and wapiti ranchers."

"Whoah." Bridget gave her a crooked smile. The Wildlife casinos made a big deal out of never serving beef or chicken or anything else usually domesticated. They also, making less of a big deal, didn't serve wild caught animals, either. They'd taken off, too; there were Wildlife casinos in Atlantic City and Monte Carlo and Hong Kong.

"No wonder you had the money to build a football team."

Bridget suddenly went still, looking intently about. "It's... let's not discuss that sort of thing out in the open. C'mon, the door's this way," she said, speeding them up. She had her keys out and opened the door. "Guests first," she said, waiving Angela in before her. She looked around before she entered the house, whispering something under her breath as she reset the alarm.

Angela looked at her oddly. What had spooked Bridget? She'd always seemed self reliant and unafraid of just about anything. Or... was it that Bridget was concerned less for her own safety than Angela's? Oh well. Bridget pulled out some fruit and nuts and those candied insects she liked so much. They got their packs out on the table and pulled out their notes and began studying, with quizzing of each other and answering of practice test questions. When it got later, Dr. Sullivan invited Angela to stay for supper, and Mom and Dad were fine with it. Fortunately, Dr. Sullivan's tastes ran to turkey burgers and vegetables, not candied bugs. Bridget grinned at that comment.

Seth walked past the open window of the biology lab covered in water and what looked like mud. Only it didn't smell like mud. He looked furious.

"Hah! Serves him right!"

"Who? Seth? What's your problem with Seth?

"My problem? You want to know what my problem with that creep is?" Angela spluttered.

"Since I asked the question, yes. It seems more polite than trying to read your mind."

Angela paid no attention to the second sentence. She was getting used to odd references like that from some people. "My problem is that he felt me up when I was out after the bus crash. Hand down my bra and everything."

"Oh, sorry. That was you? I've heard various stories but never quite put the two of you together." She went back to the lab notebook, filling in observations from the microscope. "You know, that really doesn't sound like Seth, though."

"What do you mean, that doesn't sound like him?"

"Well, I met him on the kindergarten playground at Dixie, y'know. He was pretty shy even then, but we got to be friends. But anyway, the nine of us were at the beach last July and when everyone else was off in the water he was sitting there under an umbrella reading a book when I needed to refresh the sun goop." She waved a pale hand. "I burn like crazy if I don't keep it on. He had a panic attack when I asked him to spread some on my back!" Angela giggled. "So it's kinda hard for me to see him feeling you, who he barely knows, up without permission when he had that much trouble even touching *me* with permission."

"Well I hope who ever did that to him doesn't get caught," Angela said as she turned back to the microscope. Bridget muttered something.

"What was that? I didn't hear you."

"I hope they do. Whatever happened on that bus I like Seth." Angela looked at her, and got a bland face in reply. She was sure that wasn't what Bridget had muttered. She was absolutely positive that she'd said, "I hope they're still alive."

Water Lilies Hospice was a good-sized place where the terminally ill waited. They'd already decided that there should be no attempt to resuscitate them if they died. Angela's grandmother Fujimori was here. She'd had a long, full life, from the World War II internment camps to seeing her granddaughter play football. Well, Angela grinned at the thought, maybe the last wasn't so important. Still, though, she came here often.

"Good afternoon, Angela," said Nurse Shubert at the front desk. "You know the drill."

"Yep." She signed herself in, and who she'd come to see. It had been a couple of weeks since she'd been here with everything going on. The place was painted pleasantly, with pictures of ponds and water lilies all over. It was soothing, a calming effect, to help the residents. Many of them knew Angela.

"Good afternoon, Angela:" Mrs. Stein greeted her. She wore a flower print dress under her mustard yellow sweater, her gray hair under a blue beret. "Are you dating that quarterback of yours yet?" Mrs. Stein had been asking that ever since she'd found out Angela was playing on the team.

"No, Mrs. Stein. Thank you for asking," Angela replied. It was a game between them.

"Why ever not? Where's he going to find a girl who likes football as much as you do?"

"Sacking him on a safety blitz in practice. I have mentioned Dani before, haven't I?" she asked with a somewhat rueful smile.

"Oh, fiddlesticks! Throwing the ball to YOU keeps him from getting sacked, doesn't it? If you're not dating him, how about one of the tight rear ends?"

"Mrs. Stein!" She exclaimed. She'd never gone there before. She felt her cheeks heat, and she felt like bolting.

"Oh, sorry I embarrassed you, dear. As I remember high school, the football players got snapped up by girls fairly quickly. If you want one for your own, you'd better act fast!"

"I have one of my own—ME!" she responded firmly.

"Well, that's true, and a girl as pretty as you won't have much trouble in finding whatever boy she likes. Or do you prefer girls? People are a lot more open about that sort of thing nowadays."

"Mrs. Stein!" she exclaimed again. "I'm going to go visit with my grandmother now."

"Have a good visit dear. I think the new boy just brought her medicine<" Mrs. Stein said with a glint in her eye.

"New boy?"

"Yes, we've had a new volunteer start. Very smart boy. Always interested to hear how it was, the real stories of people. So many young people don't take the time to listen, but this boy does. I heard your grandmother talking to him about the camps. And she talks to him about you quite a bit, too. On the football team! She's very proud of you, you know. She'll be even prouder when you make Honor Roll, too."

"Thanks." She walked down the corridor to her grandmother's room. Her grandmother roomed with Mrs. Royce, so her room was decorated half with the rose patterns her grandmother loved and half with Mrs. Royce's Parisian street scenes. She knocked at the door, hearing her grandmother talking about events when she was in high school, and called out "Granma? Hi, it's me Angela!"

"Oh, come in darling! I was just talking with this nice young man. He brought me my afternoon pill and…" She stumbled to a halt as the two young people stared at each other. "Oh, you know him! Delightful."

"Unfortunately not, Mrs. Fujimori. I am compelled by court order to stay at least fifty feet away from your granddaughter. I shall therefore depart," Seth said. He took the tray with him, the crystal headed flashlight on a chain around his neck dimming as he left.

"What the hell are you doing here?"

"Angela! Language!" her grandmother said.

"Community service, Miss Fujimori. Please excuse me. I have rounds on the other side of the hospice," Seth edged around her and departed.

"Angela that was no way to treat someone on staff here. What were you thinking?"

"Granma, that's the boy who put his hand down my bra in August. How do you expect me to treat him?"

"And he's been punished by the courts for doing so. He treated you politely here and obeyed his sentence. You could consider doing the same rather than indulging in such language. We raised you better than that," her grandmother replied. "He's been polite and humble here. In fact, he's been willing to sit and listen to us, talk to us, more than most attendants or family visiting only out of duty. I know you don't like him. What he did was wrong. But he seems genuinely interested in correcting his behavior. It seems that you calling him on it will make him a better man."

Angela sniffed.

"Well, tell me how school is going, if you'd rather not talk about that," Granma said.

"Pretty well. We're on course for the county championships. I've got a brilliant lab partner, Bridget, in biology, and our study sessions have helped me get A's on the tests. Geometry isn't going so well, but I've got a study group there too, just not as brilliant. I've got an English Lit class and a Standard English class, and those are both going well, we're reading Shakespeare in English Lit—sonnets at the moment, and we're needing to write our own on similar themes."

"Oh? When do I get to hear it?"

"When it's done, Granma! When it's done! Anyway, Spanish is OK. So's history. We're still learning the basics in Spanish, and world history we're into the age of empires, so we're looking at Rome and India and China and Persia. Music we're learning theory and will be figuring out what instruments we want to learn starting in the spring."

"What are you thinking about?"

"I've got it narrowed down to guitar or drums. I'm not sure which."

"How much do you want to drive your parents nuts?" she asked with a conspirator's gleam in her eyes.

"Granma!" she said, delightfully scandalized. She knew Dad didn't want her having this conversation.

"Drums are worse than guitar. Way worse, from a parent's perspective," Granma continued.

"Well, then drums. Definitely drums."

"Hey, Ange!" Bridget greeted her as she sat down at the bench for lab. "What are you up to this weekend?"

"We don't have a game Friday night, I've got no tests or papers due next week, so I was just going to vege and watch football. Why? What's up?"

"Mom's attending a conference at Humboldt State, and I was wondering if you'd like to come with us. Arcata's beautiful."

"Humboldt State? I dunno, Bridget. I mean, we're only freshmen. College isn't anywhere close." Visiting a college campus? Really, what for?

"Not what Mom says, and anyway, that's the excuse for parents." They grinned at each other. Getting serious about college was something just about all parents could be counted on to support. "More to the point, Keisha told me you know about the new league. The Unicorns are having tryouts this weekend, and I'd like your thoughts. So you game?"

Ange stared at her for a few minutes. "Let me get this straight. You want me to come with you to evaluate players for your football team. You're not asking about a fantasy league, either. An actual football team."

"Yeppers! A girls' weekend. Whaddya say?"

"I'm in. Let me check with the old folks, though, and I'll get back to you."

"Fabulous! Friday after school."

"Perfect! I think I can put a bag into my locker. If not, my gym locker will work."

The trip to Arcata was up Highway 1, which meant it was scenic through the redwoods and along the coast. It was also a LONG drive. Angela did some listening to music on her phone, chatted with Bridget and her mother, listened to some more music, played highway games. Dr. Sullivan proved to be intelligent and knowledgeable… at least about what interested her. She let Bridget and Angela pick radio stations for the drive, but kept asking who was playing. She'd tap along to the music on the steering wheel; she just didn't know who was who. Field research apparently didn't leave a lot of time for music.

When she wasn't chatting, Bridget was obviously reading something on her tablet. After they got to the hotel—there was a trundle bed; Bridget ended up getting the low straw—she asked what Bridget had been reading. Maybe the book would be worth reading herself on the way back. She was floored when Bridget replied she'd been reading the Journal of Modern Genetics.

"Why would you be reading something like that? I thought you were reading a novel! Or maybe something for English."

"Well, the more you know, the more you can do, if you take my meaning. There were some fascinating articles on rewilding and rebreeding quaggas." She paused. "I'm not sure there's sufficient diversity in local populations of jaguars and grizzlies to really work to bring back a genetically distinct California version, so maybe multiple strains?"

"Bridget, I know you've been helping me a lot with bio, and I understood all the words, but I'm really not sure what you were talking about with that last sentence."

"Hmm? Oh! I was talking about rewilding California—bringing back species that used to live here, specifically jaguars and grizzly bears. I find the concept fascinating," Bridget replied.

"Oh, OK. Yeah, that does sound pretty cool." She paused. "Did Keisha make you THAT kind of money?

"Oh, ah, no. Especially not after I had to put the college fund money back into the accounts. But she still has plenty to play with, and I have every confidence that by the time we graduate high school we'll have plenty."

The next day dawned overcast and breezy. They both wore sweaters and jeans out to the practice field, but where Bridget opted for some light braiding and free hair under her baseball cap Angela tied hers back in a ponytail.

The women trying out for the Unicorns were working out at Humboldt State University. The Lumberjacks' football field made for an excellent trial ground. The women were working out without pads, of course. "How did you determine the skill sets?"

"Well, we mostly just stole from the NFL. We didn't see any particular reason to reinvent the football. Whether we keep it that way we'll see, but it seemed a good starting point." Bridget replied in her sunglasses and hat. Despite the clouds she'd still slathered on the suntan lotion. Dr. Sullivan had dropped them off at the field and gone to give her speech on the ecology of steelhead runs. Two large white horses had been fitted with "unicorn horns" and trotted up and down the side of the field, and several other big horses—without the jewelry—stood around waiting for their turns.

"Miss Sullivan, thank you for coming," said the woman in charge of the horses. "Any of these fellows tickle your fancy?" she said, gesturing to the horses. Bridget and Angela greeted each of the beautiful horses in turn, getting their hands lipped and their hair snuffled as the horses seemed just as eager to be selected the official "Unicorn" of Arcata as any of the women out on the field wanted to be on the first team. Angela didn't know what breeds they were and didn't care. They were friendly and affectionate.

"Angela, do you ride?" Bridget asked.

"Not very well," she admitted. One of the horses seemed to have claimed her, nuzzling at her neck and lipping her ear. She giggled at the tickling sensation. "Football and volleyball and swimming took up most of my time, and karate and singing lessons took up a lot of the rest. Mom wanted a choirgirl."

"Well, miss, Marshmallow here is a gentle boy, and he seems to like you, so why don't you climb up into his saddle?" the woman said. The horse nodded his head repeatedly, as if he understood exactly what the woman had said. Angela hugged the great white head, and somehow got the sense that the horse had winked at Bridget. But she got into the saddle and took the reins, and looked over to where Bridget was already comfortably seated.

"Come on! Last time I had a good ride was with Seth."

"Seth? Really, he rides?"

"Don't let that belly of his fool you. He's even got a horse of his own. Named the poor thing "Orcinus", of course, but damn he's a fine horse. C'mon, I want to go watch the quarterbacks." She clicked to her mount and they rode off.

"I don't suppose you heard and will just follow?" Angela imitated the clicking and tapped at her mount's side, and they followed Bridget to where the quarterbacks were working out. There were five of them, and a coach. "Who do you have as your starting quarterback?" Angela asked as she caught up to where Bridget was. Bridget was still in the saddle.

"Andrea Jepson. She's from Pennsylvania, so I don't know if you've heard about her, but she did very well back east, and we're lucky to have her. She's the one working out with the receivers over there."

"What's so lucky about her?

"Some of the others don't even have a starting quarterback yet, so they're working the receivers out with whoever they can get. Some of them have to use guys throwing the ball." She smirked. "I heard that Alex is throwing the ball to receivers himself."

Angela giggled at that. "Can I catch a few passes?"

"Coach Ramirez? My friend Angela here would like to catch a few passes. She plays receiver on our high school team. Would that be alright or would it throw things off too much?" She asked the heavy-set young man working the quarterbacks on their drills.

"It's alright with me. Ladies? Want to throw to a live target for a bit?" The women trying out for the quarterback spots nodded and smiled at her. She got her routes and ran down the field for each participant, caught the ball, ran back and flipped it to the next woman in line. After catching the passes, "You're a lot more accurate than most of the passes I've tried to catch. So many of them think I'm several inches taller than I am." The quarterbacks chuckled. While Angela was having her fun, Bridget was quietly conferring with Coach Ramirez. He kept his eyes on the quarterbacks and their throws, but was still talking shop with the youthful owner of the team.

Angela and Bridget rode over to where the wide receivers were working out with Andrea Jepson and another coach. Angela once again dismounted, and this time Bridget joined her. "Good morning, Ms. Jepson, Coach Kendrick," Bridget said.

"Good morning, Miss Sullivan. How are you today?"

"Very well, and yourselves?" She looked at the horses. "Don't wander too far." They nodded.

"It's uncanny how they obey verbal commands from you like that," Andrea said. Bridget smiled and shrugged. Marshmallow snuffled a bit more in Angela's raven locks. She turned to glare at the horse.

"My hair is not grass!" she said to the horse. He put his nose to her cheek in apology and wandered over to the side of the field where the grass was longer and began snacking. Bridget's horse remained by her side, looking over her shoulder as she conferred with Coach Kendrick. Bridget absently stroked his head and cheek.

There was a sudden whinny of challenge from Marshmallow. Six large brindled dogs with slavering mouths and gleaming eyes, almost glowing, were coming from the woods on the far side of the stadium. Marshmallow and the other horse both charged towards the dogs, with out any seeming thought for themselves. The hounds bayed as if they'd found their quarry, and the horses smashed into them. The dogs weren't interested in horseflesh, however, but two were speared by the decorative horns that Bridget had on their bridles. Apparently those things were sturdier than they looked, because the horses reared up and tossed the speared dogs before bringing their hooves crashing down again. The thrown dogs crashed into the stands, but got up. They were bleeding from where the horns had pierced them and from where they'd been cut on the stands, but they got up and kept coming. Marshmallow's right fore hoof smashed one dog's skull and it went down, unmoving. The horse—er, stallion, they were both stallions, she finally noticed fought with wild eyed fury, lashing out at the dogs. The dogs seemed confused, for Bridget's mount was pressing his attack as well, foregoing the horn to use it's hooves, forced to battle the horses when they were trying to get to the field. The stallions looked like they were fighting *together*, each facing the other's rump so no dog could get past them and bite at their flanks. A dog leaped at Marshmallow's side and met the other stallion's hoof. Angela winced as it's ribcage crumpled and the dog lay whimpering and gathering itself until one of Marshmallow's rear hooves came down on it's head.

The remaining four dogs tried to circle the horses, get around them to the field beyond where people were getting out of the way—Bridget and Angela were staying together with Ms. Jepson and Coach Kendrick and the wide receivers while the stunned stable people were grabbing for tools and the trank gun and headed over to the combat. But they had no clear shot on the dogs as against the horses. But the horses weren't panicking, they were fighting, and even as Angela watched one of them dispatched another dog with its rear hoof. The other horses had been corralled away from the fighting by the time the stable people got over to it, but the two stallions seemed to have it well in hoof. A fourth dog went down forever and the stallions separated again to eliminate the final two... oddly enough with horns to the skulls.

"Wow. What just happened?" Angela asked.

"There have been reports of a pack of feral dogs around for the past week or so. I guess they decided to attack. But those stallions of yours, Miss Sullivan, are exceptional animals. I don't think they have anything like a pureblood lineage but anyone would be glad to talk to you about stud. Those are some smart, and brave, horses."

Bridget smiled at the man who'd stepped up to her. "Coach Simpson, I couldn't agree more with that description. And I think those two have just cemented their places as official unicorns of the team. Oh, Coach

Simpson, Angela Fujimori. Angela's a receiver on our high school team. Angela, Coach Jonathan Simpson, head coach of the Arcata Unicorns."

"Pleased to meet you, Miss Fujimori. I hope we'll be giving you a tryout in seven-eight years?" he said, white teeth flashing in his dark face.

"Ah, thank you," she replied blushing. "I look forward to it. But who knows? One of the other teams might give me a better offer!"

"That's a possibility of course, but in that case you need to talk to your friend here. I saw you out there catching balls for fun. But what did you think of the quarterbacks?"

"You're seriously asking me? I mean, I'm only fourteen!"

"It's what I invited you up here for, remember! And as for only being fourteen, how old do you think *I* am?" Bridget put in with a smile. The breeze blew her hair out.

"The first quarterback, Jessica, was pretty good. Center of my chest, no difficulties catching it. It had a good amount of power behind it, too. The second, Caitlin, was ever better. Dropped it right where I could catch it but a corner behind me couldn't unless she had a lot of height on me. Kathryn and Barbara, unfortunately, weren't quite as good. I had to reach for the pass Barbara threw, and Kathryn's had lost a lot of power by the time it got to me. I don't think her arm strength is what it could be."

"Ok, thanks. Did you have much of an opportunity to watch the receivers or cornerbacks?"

"Some, before those rabid dogs came in. Of the receivers, I think your best bets are Jones, Gadowski, and Miernik. They looked like they ran the best with the best hands, anyway. I particularly liked Miernik's sudden cuts once she had the ball. That was really good. They also seemed to show the best evasions.

"On the cornerbacks, I tend to think tall and athletic give me the most problems. Granted I'm playing with boys, and most of them are older so most of them are going to be taller than me anyway. They're also going to likely be able to bring me down if they can get their hands on me in the first place. I can be big, strong, and tough, but odds are they're going to be bigger and stronger than I'm ever going to be. So if a corner's going to stop me, they need to catch me in the first place. Of the corners I saw out there, I liked Silverstein, O'Connor, Ali, and Lo the best in terms of building a team. They looked like the best ones to actually catch a receiver."

He nodded thoughtfully. "Okay, thank you. I see why Miss Sullivan wanted you up here taking a look at the team for her. If you were older than fourteen I'd be strongly suggesting that she hire you as a scout. Keep going and keep thinking."

Alex's house! Site of the great Halloween party. Dad dropped her, Liz, and Carmen off. Angela straightened her hair buns and the belt of her Princess Leia costume while Liz in her "bloodstained" "psycho-surgeon" hospital scrubs and Carmen in her Carmen Sandiego red hat and overcoat waited, and they walked up the creaking steps. The hanging spiders and glowing eyed rats and the gravestones looked almost real and the dry ice in water pumped out plenty of mist. The door seemed to open on it's own when they walked in. Alex had really gone all out!

She passed a number of her teammates—one guy dressed as his cheerleader girlfriend, one guy as a pocket-protector wearing nerd, one guy dressed as Chewbacca, a couple of vampires, Frankenstein, some random masks, Zorro, Batman, Wolverine, Superman, Zeus, Tarzan, one guy not even trying in a domino mask and normal clothes--before she saw Alex. "Wow," she breathed to Liz and Carmen, "And Dad wouldn't even consider me in slave Leia!"

Alex was bare chested, with armbands, a crown, a cape, and a loincloth, all enhanced with iridescent feathers (mostly blue). Swinging from his belt was a wooden Aztec sword. She couldn't tell if it was authentically set with bits of obsidian or not.

"How'd he stop you?"

"Money. He wouldn't buy it." She was still staring at Alex, barely noticing the crowned mummy and Greek girl talking to him. "Damnit, Lord Huitzilapoca, you should have told me," the mummy said. He tucked the crook and flail into a cleverly disguised belt. He turned to the three girls, a funeral mask covering his face and an ankh gleaming on his chest, bowed slightly and said, "Highness, I apologize. I had not known you would be present and will immediately depart. Enjoy the party, please."

"Lord Osiris, you know what is…" The girl said

"Lady Hecate, I am bound to leave," he interrupted her. He gestured at Alex. "Our little hummingbird forgot that." He strode toward the door. "Should you need my aid, call and I shall return. Otherwise…" A sensation went through her, and she shivered. Goosebumps all over her body, her hair trying to stand on end. The mummy looked at Alex and the Greek girl. "Did you two feel that?"

"Feel what?" Carmen asked, perplexed. "I didn't feel anything."

"Neither did I," Liz said.

"I did feel something weird," Angela said..

The three kids dressed as gods looked at each other. "You two head to the front and check it out, then come back here, we'll need you as reserves." Alex took out a microphone. The mummy pulled the crook and flail out of his belt and went towards the door, the Greek girl pulling out and lighting a torch and a key. "Everyone, the time for dungeon festivities has begun! Please go below!" Almost everyone was crowding towards the stairs down. Kids dressed as Mother Nature, Satan, Neptune, Amerastu, Pan, and the statue of liberty stayed up stairs, though. Angela was swept along down to the cellars.

She didn't stay there, though. The more interesting things were happening back upstairs, and she wanted to go find out what was happening. No one else seemed remotely interested in doing so, though. It was just going to be up to her to find out for herself, so she went on back up the stairs and looked. Greek girl and Osiris were standing around near the front doors. They weren't talking, or at lest not to each other. It looked as if they were listening to conversations, though. She saw Osiris raise a hand to his ear. While they were distracted she went out a back door.

Alex's house was fairly large. Nowhere near the size of Bridget's place, but still a couple stories high on a hill with a pool in back and tall trees around it. Around the house was some sort of light show, with swirling clouds and heavy with the smell of impending rain. Lighting crackled in the sky, and the thunder made it obvious just how close it was. Other flashes looked and sounded like sudden explosions, but didn't seem to be actually lighting anything on fire—and they came in all the colors of the rainbow, more like fireworks than real explosions. She remembered from an old chemistry set that different chemicals could be used to create different colored flames, but damned if she remembered what did what.

The light show wasn't the only strange thing going on. Howlings in the night filled the air, and they weren't coyotes. She'd heard coyotes before and these were different. Bigger, deeper, more menacing than any coyote ever howled. And they weren't hounds either. She was pretty sure of that. Whatever they were they sent a chill down her spine. A fresh light seemed to gleam along the fence line, as if someone were defending the house and all within it, and then things got through. Well, not things. People in costumes, with murder in their hearts and in their minds. Angela rushed out to face one, a guy in a goblin mask and he went down to the karate she'd been learning ever since she was little. She followed that kick with another to the face and he stopped moving.

Someone in a gorilla costume and football uniform charged her, knocking her down. It wasn't a tackle, it wasn't a move out of any martial art. He simply used his greater strength and size to knock her down, and her attempt to trip him went nowhere. The gorilla of the gridiron raised a rock to smash on her head when he suddenly stiffened and fell over.

Mother Nature was standing over her, an overflowing horn of plenty on her back and a leaf entwined stick in her hand. "Princess, you shouldn't be out here. For your own safety get back to the party." The trees were blocking her view of the lightshow on the other side, but it was continuing. Something fell out of the sky and smashed heavily into the ground, crumpling rather than exploding like in the movies almost like the plane crashing into the church, while more lights came from the other side of the house. "We'll be in soon enough. Well, most of us. Lord Osiris is leaving as soon as his business here is done."

"I don't know what you're doing out here, but I want to help." She smiled briefly, gesturing with the "blaster" she'd brought along. "Even if this is a prop gun."

"Princess, thank you for the offer, but you'd just distract us. You're not part of the plan. We'd have to protect you, and we can't really afford the distraction," Mother Nature replied. "Please, return to the party. Lord Osiris is taking my place while I get you back inside, but that's really not a good thing."

"Come on, really, what's going…" She suddenly felt her guts unclench, and she needed, really needed to get to the bathroom before they emptied.

She ran back in desperate to reach a toilet. Behind her, Mother Nature gave a crooked smile and returned to her position.

∞•◦◦❂◦◦•∞

She came out of the bathroom maybe twenty minutes later, when she finally felt secure. Alex looking tired (and bleeding from a dozen scrapes), but triumphant. "With one exception, Angela, the others have rejoined the party," Alex said. "They are all unaware of what occurred. As far as they know, all of us were down there with them."

"And you'll do something to me if I say otherwise?" she said apprehensively. Movies and TV suggested that the next thing the people with the secret would do is make sure that no one was in a position to report the truth.

Alex grinned, then laughed. "Not at all. This is a friendly warning." The wooden Aztec maca was now bright red. "But just who do you think will believe you?"

"Ah…" she stopped. She couldn't actually think of anyone who might believe what she could actually tell. Lights? Noises? Guys in gorilla and goblin costumes? No one would equate that to anything mysterious.

"That's what I thought. Ange, we hold no animosity towards you. We're certainly not mad at you or threatening you. Those of us who really know you like you and consider you a friend. Well, Lord Osiris isn't quite like that, but he doesn't hate you, either. Consider it some enchanted evening, perhaps." He grinned at her. "I'll throw you more passes?"

"You think you can bribe me with football?"

He chuckled. "No, probably not. But that doesn't mean I won't bend efforts to helping you become even more of a star of the team than you already are. Just because you're my friend. Someday I may even tell you what happened here tonight. It simply won't be now."

The Monday after the Halloween party, Angela arrived at school to find a massive bouquet of orange and black flowers and a box of See's candies in her locker, along with a hand written note, "Thanks for a Great Halloween! Did that REALLY happen?" decorated with a grinning jack-o-lantern. It was signed with the gods' names from the party. OK, she guessed. I don't really know what was going on, no one will believe me—Alex was right about that--and they're being nice about it.

Oscar Jimenez came up to Angela as she was leaving Mr. Curley's English class. This one wasn't as interesting as Ms. Gonzalez' class; here they were diagramming sentences and other boring stuff rather than reading Shakespeare. If it was old and hard to understand, at least it could be fun. And Hamlet was next! "Hi Oscar. What's up?"

"Um, I was wondering if you… um, got the homework in Ms. Bissaro's class?" he mumbled.

"Yeah, sure," she said, checking her phone. "It's pages 297 to 316, and the questions at the back."

"Thanks, Angela." He opened his mouth as if he was going to say something else and then closed it and went to his next class.

Carmen and Karen giggled. "He's not very good at asking someone out, is he?" Karen asked.

Angela smiled. "No, but he's a geek. I wouldn't have said yes, but I would have let him down easy. He's fairly nice."

"Since we all know where your heart truly lies," Teddy Pope interjected, taking a seat for the next class. He gave her a smile when she glared at him.

"Will you give that a rest?" Angela said. Unfortunately, neither Seth nor Alex nor Bridget were around to jerk Teddy up short, and he'd displayed a remarkable lack of willingness to pay much attention to anyone else. A teacher might get him to pay attention, but not other students.

"C'mon, Ange, we need to get to bio," Carmen said, tugging at her sleeve. She was right. Bio was half way across the school, too, so they really needed to get going.

"He won't wait forever, you know! Better make up your little spat before he goes looking for a real girl!" Teddy called after them.

"Why are you blushing, Ange? You're not really taking anything that ass said seriously, are you?" Karen asked as they cruised down the hallways.

"Sometimes it gets to me, y'know? I don't like him. He doesn't like me. I know he lied to the court and to Ms. Lee. But Alex says he'd asked him to help me on the bus, and that's why he was touching me at all. And I know Alex didn't actually see anything, that he couldn't. But it's been months, and he served the time. And when Teddy starts in on me with that stuff *he* tells Teddy to knock it off. And, God help me, he met my grandmother in the hospice where he's doing his community service and she actually *likes* him! What if he was trying to help me, or was trying to in addition to coping a feel?"

"You've got it confusingly bad," Carmen said consolingly, as they slid to a halt at Mrs. Kravitz's classroom. "Well, time to watch Bridget blow the curve some more!"

"It's not just Bridget, you know, Carmen," Karen said. "Malcolm and Angela are right behind her blowing their own holes in it. They're just not as noisy about it."

"Yeah, I know. When did YOU get so good at biology?" Carmen asked.

"Since I got assigned Bridget as a lab partner," she replied. "I think just about anyone would be good with her as your lab partner."

Angela was headed to the grove of valley oaks to study history—no one else was available, but they did have that test this afternoon—when she heard the voices. She recognized two of them. "Toranos, I've been attacked by them repeatedly over the past few weeks, and it needs to stop." That was Seth, and he sounded angry.

"I'm sorry about that, Thantoris. Really. I'll talk to them." Alex? What was with the weird names?

"Do more than TALK, Toranos," Seth replied… and it was a demand.

"I don't think you're quite getting it, Toranos. Thantoris hasn't defended himself. Not yet. Not beyond what might be reasonably expected. But these are your friends, not his. You know perfectly well he doesn't like them…" That was a girl, but she wasn't sure who it was. Not someone she talked to much, anyway. But after the homecoming dance, she winnowed her way… that wasn't Bridget, or Keisha. It didn't sound like Jennifer. That left Dawn. Dawn Takugawa.

"They're assholes. And I am done putting up with them. They come after me again and I DO defend myself. Your precious team will never be the same." Angela blanched at that.

"Wait, wait, Thantoris. No need to do anything rash. They're mad about what Ange's saying about you," Alex was pleading with Seth.

"I know that…"

"Thantoris, please. You asked me to help and I will." Angela thought the girl was drawing in a breath. "As he said, Toranos, he knows why your friends are angry with him. That said, both you and he know it's just plain wrong. Chiomara has been doing her best, but it is high time that YOU took a stand. For his sake and the sake of your friends." Her voice lowered. "All of us know it's wrong, Toranos. Even Angoral. Even you," her voice lowered even more. "And you know what Thantoris can do. We had graphic demonstrations already this year. You know as well as I that is what he will do, if this keeps up."

"I am NOT willing to forgive and forget, Toranos. I am willing to stay my hand if the attacks *cease*."

Angela heard Alex gulp. "Alright, Thantoris, Grianne. The attacks will stop. You have my word. You've got a list of those who came after you?"

"I do. Your copy." Seth still sounded angry.

"I'll take care of it, Thantoris. Today." Alex was turning on her?

"Toranos. If I am attacked after today, I will defend myself."

Angela heard them start to get up, and decided that she didn't really want them to know she'd been listening. She hid behind one of the trees, and watched as Seth, Alex, and Dawn left the grove. Seth's hair was wet again. No, wait, it was dry. Wasn't it wet a second ago?

As the JV squad was sitting and chatting and waiting for Coach to come in and make his usual pre-practice speech on goals for this practice, Alex stood up and rapped his knuckles on the little table in the front of the room. Everyone sort of looked up. Angela nearly buried her face in her hands. This was it.

"Hey guys. I need to talk to you about something."

"What's up, Alex? You getting sacked too much?" David Smith asked with a smirk.

"No, this is serious, and it concerns you, Dave. We all know what happened to Ange after the bus crash. And I'm sure Coach would be happy about you standing up for your teammate." Huh?

"But attacking Seth Dupree isn't helping anything. He's ready to go to Coach, and the Principal, and the cops about it. Leave the guy alone. He's already on community service. He's already apologized. He's done his time in Juvie. He's been told to stay away from her and he has."

"Oh, come on, Alex! I know the little shit's a friend of yours from way back. But we haven't really done much more than mess with him. After what he did to Ange, he deserves a lot more. And I say we give it to him!" Kevin Pastorini said. The rumble of agreement was obvious, and nearly unanimous.

Mike Wu spoke up. "I think Alex has a point. It'd be one thing to support Ange in a fresh confrontation with him. But we're starting to be the assholes here." Keisha's influence, probably.

Angela couldn't help but think on what she'd heard in the grove. What did Dawn mean about what Seth was capable of? And what he would do? Going to the principal and Coach was one thing, going to the cops was another, but Dawn seemed to have been stressing something a lot darker. Maybe even violent, some form of direct action on Seth's part that would leave the team... what? Someone with Seth's belly wasn't going to be a black belt; she knew that from her own karate lessons. Did Seth have a gun?

Angela stood. They were doing this "for" her. She couldn't let her teammates get shot because of her. She started to speak. "Thanks for having my back, guys, but Coach explained the rules at the beginning of the first practice. You get caught bullying and you're off the team and not getting back on it. You get accused of bullying and you're off the team until they've investigated it. I don't like Seth and I think he got off far too lightly. But payback's MINE to deliver, OK, guys?" She looked around at everyone, and there was a brief chorus of agreement.

"Ok, that's all I wanted to say. Hi, Coach." Coach Nyugen walked in, thanking Alex and then launching into his normal speech. Angela paid it little attention.

"Mind if I sit with you today, Ange?" She looked up in the cafeteria to see Alex standing there, a burger and fries on his lunch tray. She'd parked herself off in a corner because she didn't really want to be with anyone today, not after that meeting before practice yesterday.

"Ok, I guess," she replied, trying to put it in a way that would get him to leave. He didn't pick up on it.

"Great!" He sat down and took a bite of his burger. "I wanted to thank you for what you said yesterday before practice. It really helped."

"Well, I couldn't let the little perve come after my team with a gun, now could I?" she said.

Alex frowned and swallowed the bite he'd just taken. "Gun? He doesn't have a gun. His parents won't let water guns in the house, let alone the real thing. Why do you think he's got a gun?"

"Then what's he capable of and will do if this keeps up?" she demanded before she took a bite of her spaghetti. "Really, Alex. You sounded scared about what he might do, and grabbing a gun and shooting up the team is about the worst I can think he'd be able to do."

"I wondered if you'd admit you heard that." He paused and took another bite. "Ange, most people probably don't see it, since the school is big enough that we don't share a lot of classes and all of us aren't in a single class. But there are nine kids who have perfect GPAs. Nine freshmen. Seth is one of them. Do you remember him offering to replace the fine sports drink we normally have at games with a powerful laxative? He's fully capable of doing that." He ate a French fry. "If you heard that part, you heard the rest of what Dawn said. Seven of them are in Seth's corner.

Think about what eight geniuses could do in retaliation if they put their minds to it."

"Eight? You said there were…" Her eyes opened wide. He had said "us".

"You got it. I'm number nine. And the laxative thing was just Seth off the top of his head."

Angela took another bite. "And you're still insisting that he wasn't copping a feel on me? Really, Alex, how can you defend him? His hand was under my…"

"Bra. You know it, you've said it. He admits it. But I've known Seth since preschool, Ange. He said he was trying to help you." He looked very serious. "His hand was there for how long? I'm not saying he's a perfectly honest person, Ange. He's not."

"I can't believe you're turning on me, Alex!"

"I'm not. Ange, please, listen." His voice took on a slightly more insistent quality, and she sat back, almost against her will, to listen to Alex. "I'm between two friends here. I've heard what you said. I've heard what he said. I know what I asked him to do. He's quiet about it, but I know his first action is to help. I've bled on him enough while he patched me up.

"He lied about what he was doing with you. I know he did, and I know why. No one would believe the truth. I also know you're wrong about what he was doing. About what he was doing for you because I asked him to do it." She sat there, understanding that Alex believed what he was saying. Was SHE wrong? Did she misinterpret what happened, misunderstand Seth's intentions? ".

"If you're on my side, answer a question. What's with the weird names you call each other? And who's 'Angoral'? Or "Felarie"? or "Chiomara"?"

He considered her for a bit, then clearly made a decision, and his voice was low. "I have gotten a lot of flack for letting you listen in on us. Dawn and Seth were not at all happy, Angoral even less so. Outsiders aren't supposed to know our secret names, much less who is who. They think that if I had wanted to tell you my name, that's my business, just like it would be Seth's if he had chosen to tell you his, but I also set it up so you know two of the rest of us. It would be a lot better for us if you just remembered us as Alex and Dawn and Seth. Certainly in any discussion you might have with someone else."

"Alex, you're still not telling me. After Halloween I know there's something else going on."

"Ange, it's better for YOU if you don't know what happened on Halloween. We arranged things so no one would know what happened, and we'd prefer things stayed that way. We have our reasons."

"Like what?" she demanded. "If you want me to play along with this you'll need to convince me."

He considered her carefully for several moments. "Angela, you're going to think I'm being as pretentious as Seth. But I'm not free to share this stuff. I've already pissed off eight people. They think I betrayed a trust simply in arranging for you to hear that conversation.

"If you really want to know about Halloween... lets just say that certain people took a dislike to some of us over the summer, and we decided to lure them into a trap that night. It worked, and they won't be bothering us or the school again. You don't need to worry about it. That's all I'm going to say on it. And since I'm fairly certain none of the people who actually do know the details are going to spill..." he shrugged, "You can complain about it until you're blue in the face. It will not help."

"And that's it? That's all you'll tell me about what's going on? Alex, Halloween's only part of it. I heard Teddy telling you something. I'm the one who found Sarah Campbell in the locker room at Homecoming. I overheard you and Seth and Teddy and Jennifer talking the day the cheerleaders were murdered. I know that something else is going on, and I want to know what."

"I know. You're not ready for it. We're not exactly ready for it, but we're already there."

"Who gave you the right to make that decision for me?"

Alex smiled. "Who gave you the right to the information? I realize you want it, but why should we give it to you? What happened at Halloween doesn't really concern you, Ange. There's no particular reason to tell you. You're not ready to believe us. So we might as well not tell you yet. At some point we will, but not yet. You're not clued in enough."

"Alex..."

"Angela, unfortunately, you're going to have to trust us. We voted whether or not to bring you in on the secret. It was seven to two against telling you."

"Alex, I trust you, personally. I don't trust Seth. I know Dawn by sight only, and I don't even know who else is involved. Trust isn't something I feel for your group." Problem was that Alex was stubborn. She'd seen that often enough on the field.

As he proved now. "I'm sorry you feel that way, Angela. What you're asking for I'm not going to give. Not yet.

She poked around her spaghetti. "Can you give me some reason to trust you guys? Something at all?"

"Whether you know it or not, we've saved your life four times this year. Not counting Halloween." He popped the last of his burger in his mouth, flashed his eyebrows at her, got up and left her goggle eyed and staring.

CHAPTER

First weekend back from vacation was the New Year's Dance. It was a very rainy night in a rainy week, following a rainy December. This time Jeffrey Ito had asked Angela to the dance. He was a cornerback, so he played defense, and Angela knew him more as a guy who covered her in practice than anything else. But he was a nice guy, for the most part, so she'd said she'd go when he asked her. She'd tried to use her date with Jeff to shut Teddy up, but it didn't faze him at all. He just kept up with his insistence that she was supposed to be with Seth. As if! She shuddered at the very thought.

Jeff proved a good dancer. She was out on the floor with him almost as much as Keisha was out there with Mike Wu. Dawn had come with Julian, and they spent quite a bit of time on the floor too. Of course half the football team grabbed her for dances. It was part of what made them so much fun. She was amused to see Bridget and Alex dancing close for what everyone else thought was a fast dance. Bridget was talking low and fast, and oddly enough they seemed to be discussing the weather.

She was sitting with Carmen, Joy, and Shannon, taking a break from the dancing, when Alex approached. "Good evening, ladies," he said.

"What's up, Alex?"

"You've noticed the rain, I presume?"

Shannon snorted. "It's not like we could miss it. It's been coming down for a week."

"Precisely. It's apparently had an adverse affect on the hills. Mudslides and the like. A friend just called me and said there was an obstruction"

Carmen said, "This friend wouldn't be a creepy perverted goth named Seth, would it?"

"Does it really matter, Carmen?" Shannon asked. "Even creepy perverted Goths can be right about the weather and the mudslides. My uncle told me over Christmas about some really bad ones." There'd been heavy rains that week, too.

"It's a warning being passed on. I don't think it really matters who gave it if it's legitimate. Thank Seth for us, Alex," Joy put in. As the rain continued to pound on the roof, Alex responded.

"He thinks that it's Lucas Valley Road that's the potential problem. He suggests taking another way out of here."

"Thanks Alex," Angela said. The current song ended and another started. "Now c'mon, I haven't had a dance with you tonight!"

As the dancing went on, the rain kept coming. Bridget, Dawn, and their dates left early. Jeff and his ride got them through the streets to her home. She kissed Jeff and went in, to hear that Lucas Valley Road was out in one section and blocked in three others. Some people had been caught, but fortunately there were no deaths, and the rain had stopped as soon as the sun came up.

With the New Year, it was time to get serious about volleyball. There were enough girls who wanted to play volleyball for there to be a full league. She was a little surprised to find Keisha Johnson on the team. Keisha was of course tall, but she'd always been more of a bookworm than an athlete. But she was proving very skilled. When Angela asked, she shrugged. "My uncles and aunts and cousins like to play, and there are nets at most of our homes. We play whenever the family gets together. And since Mom is very, very competitive, she insists on regular practice at home. Gotta beat her brother Charlie!" she said with a wry smile. "I'd rather be reading or managing the financials, but Mom insists. She's already placing bets on the Sphinx games with every one of her brothers and sisters."

"When does the League start playing?"

"Middle of March. Should only be a little overlap with volleyball, and all the Sphinx games during the overlap will be within easy distance. Our four away games are in Berkeley, San Francisco, Sacramento, and Fresno, while we host Santa Cruz, Arcata, Hollywood, and San Diego. It'll work out fine.

By the time March rolled around, there was a lot of buzz about the Golden State Football League. The youthful owners managed to keep themselves hidden somehow. The few who knew who they were smirked at each other—and them—in the halls.

Angela was coming out of math when she stopped suddenly. Seth was right in front of her. He had an odd expression in his eyes. "Angela. Your grandmother asked me to tell you she misses you."

"What?"

"At Water Lilies. The hospice? Your grandmother misses you."

"Are you still there? Then I'm not going."

He closed his eyes. "I won't be there the rest of the week. You should visit her again. Before it's too late."

"What are you talking about? Dad was just there, she was fine."

"You do know what a hospice is for, don't you? To make someone as comfortable as possible while they wait for the end? What I got there is that your grandmother has a week. Maybe two. Probably not two." He hefted his pack. "I've delivered her message and my warning. Your decision is your own." They both sensed Julian Kanekawa come up.

"Seth, you aren't supposed to be bothering Angela."

"I was passing on a message, Your Highness. But I was just leaving."

"Your Highness is not a proper form of address for a Class President," he responded.

"But it is for a Prince of Hawaii." He walked past her into his own class. Julian had a look of chagrin on his face and hurried off to his own class.

Thing of it was, he was right. A hospice like Water Lilies… her grandmother could be dying. She resolved to go that very afternoon.

She rode her bike out to the hospice and parked it. She checked her grandmother's room and found she was out in one of the common areas playing pinochle. "Angela! There's my girl. Glad you could come visit me."

"Hi Granma. Sorry I haven't been recently, but I didn't want to run into that creepy Seth."

"And that's a reason not to see your grandmother?" Mrs. Stein put in. "Girl, you need to be braver than that! I know he's got power, but if he bothers you punch him in the nose!"

"Well, he was creepier than usual at school today. Said Granma had only a week or two," Angela said.

The elderly ladies fell silent and looked at each other. "I'm sorry to hear that, Helen. This place won't be the same without you," Mrs. Richmond said. The others made similar comments. Mr. Talbott came over to ask what the fuss was, and when they told him he hugged Helen Fujimori. Angela was baffled.

"It was just Seth being Seth. He's a jerk."

Mrs. Stein looked at her. "The boy KNOWS, child. He simply KNOWS. If he waffled with a maybe it's because there was a variable that hadn't been decided on yet. Otherwise he could have given you the hour. I saw him say a new arrival wouldn't last through check in and the poor man didn't. He knows."

"I know you don't like him, dear, and I know he put his hands on you back in August, but that doesn't mean he's wrong, Angie-chan." Her grandmother patted her hand. "I've had a good life. I'd have liked to live long enough to see you married, but that doesn't appear to be part of God's plan. I don't have long, so forgive me if I'm offering you advice you don't want to be hearing just yet. Find yourself a good man, Angie-chan. Someone who you can share your life with, who will stand beside you, who will always, always have your back as you have his, someone with whom you can take joy in each other. Always remember I love you, Angie-chan."

Angela went back to Water Lilies every day, even after Seth came back to work there. Her grandmother lived two more weeks. When Angela arrived in her room, the nurse had just found her. She had passed in her sleep during a nap. The tears came, and she grabbed the nearest person without being able to see whom it was, and her arms went around her, too. When she could see, she was surprised to find herself hugging Bridget, who gave her a melancholy smile. "Angela, I'm so sorry."

"Wha… wha… what are you doing here?"

"Seth. He said you'd need a friend here today."

Swim team tryouts were held in late March. Angela pulled on the straps and walked out to the big indoor pool. The other girls—including her friends Karen, Joy, Liz, and Carmen—were already out there, caps on their heads, ready to race. They were alternating with the boys, so there was a small crowd of boys trying out for the team, too. Her football team mates weren't going for swim team; baseball was much more their thing, or lacrosse. There were others watching the tryouts; Alex, for example, and a number of her friends who were cheering her on while boy watching. Alex, Teddy, and Solomon were watching the girls side and Bridget, Keisha, Dawn, and Jenny were watching the boys side. Seth was seated high in a corner on the boys' side with a pair of binoculars watching the girls' side. Creepy! Then she spotted the real reason they were here—Malcolm Muir was wearing a cap and Speedo. Where most of the boys on the team seemed skinny, Malcolm—much like Alex—had already gotten some serious musculature. He wasn't any taller than the other boys, but he had definitely filled out. So had Julian.

The suits were Lucas Valley High purple, which meant they looked almost black once they got wet. The caps were also purple, but had the lightning bolts on them to help identify the school. Not that they were wearing those yet; they'd have to purchase them once they made the team. Angela's suit was green, and her cap a washed out turquoise.

But however interesting he was to look at, she had a race. It would work like a swim meet—girls, then boys, in age brackets, in freestyle, backstroke, breast stroke, butterfly, and individual medley. Relays would be set up during the year out of the best swimmers. It was time she stepped up to the starting block. So she did. She assumed starting position, and launched herself into the water. The freestyle was a long, energetic swim, but she had won when she got back to the starting blocks. That should give her a good chance at making the team. A towel was tossed perfectly on top of her, and when she pulled it off she saw Alex give her a smile and a thumbs up. Of course he threw it properly. What good was a quarterback who couldn't throw well? She went up in the stands to talk to him and watch the next heat of the girls, since Carmen was in this one. She'd edged out Karen.

"Hi Ange. You did good in that one. Looks like you'll make the team, if you keep that up," Alex said from his vantage point.

"Are you sure you want to be over here, Angela?" Teddy asked. "Your true love is over there," he went on, pointing to Seth as if she didn't know perfectly well where he was.

"Knock it off, Teddy," Alex said.

"Before she does," Bridget put in. "You do know she does karate, right?"

"Nothing to be that afraid of, you know. I've been irritating her at speaking the truth. Those who do are often vilified." Teddy spoke in mournful tones. "Consider all the martyrs there have been who have dared to speak the gospels to the unbelievers. But I have not rendered her so beyond herself that she would assault me, I am sure."

"You DO know you're seriously irritating Seth every time you bring that up, don't you, Teddy?" Solomon put in. "Are you looking to goad *him* beyond himself? I don't think that that would be what anyone might consider a wise idea."

Teddy actually blanched at that.

"So Seth is scarier than I am, is he? I don't think I care for the sound of that," Angela said. "Go Carmen!"

"Really, Teddy, give it a rest already." Dawn said. "If they eventually hook up, good for them. If they never do, oh well. From what I'm told plenty of people don't. And your contributions don't help."

They kept watching the try-outs. A couple girls beat Angela's time, and then it was the boys' turn. Malcolm swam in the middle of the pack—it was just a luck of the draw thing—but he was far and away the best swimmer. He crushed his completion, five full seconds in front of the next fastest time, Julian's. Angela excused herself for the backstroke.

After that encounter, she stuck to where the cheerleaders were cheering their favorites on. Angela was definitely one of those. She did well in all her races. Malcolm continued with his crushing of everyone else. He was obviously going to be the star of the team. Julian was just as obviously the second best boy, and they made a point of congratulating each other.

When she was preparing for the Individual Medley, she thought she sensed Seth's appraisal of her. He was still up in his seat with his binoculars, staying well away from the pool. Probably so no one could accuse him of violating the rules about getting close to her, even if he had figured out another way to be creepy. When she looked up, though, his attention didn't seem to be on her. He wasn't even focusing on the pool! Oh, well, if he was focusing on someone else all the better. She heard the cheers, and focused on the swimming. She stopped hearing the echoes and prepared to begin.

It happened on the butterfly leg. She cramped up—arms, legs, stomach, even her neck. She couldn't move. She couldn't even turn herself over. What was wrong with her? If she couldn't turn she was going to drown! She started panicking. She felt people trying to get to her, to save her and figure out what was wrong. Suddenly as it began she was free of it. She raised her head and took a breath. Coach Adams came over to her. "Angela! Let's get you out of the water. As in NOW."

Coach Adams was a tall woman, a former competitive swimmer in her own right, with curly dark hair that she kept cut short and blue eyes, in her thirties. She was wearing purple sweats with the school's crossed lightning bolt emblem. A couple of senior boys lifted her directly out of the water, and Coach Adams had her lie down on the deck before doing a once over, checking her head for any sort of injury. "What happened? You were doing so well!"

"I cramped, Coach. All over. I don't know how or why," she told her.

"That's a weird one. You seem to be okay at the moment; at least I'm not finding anything," the coach said as she continued her examination, running her hands down her legs and arms looking for sore spots. "I think you should be checked out by a doctor to be on the safe side, though."

"How quickly does she need to get there, Coach?" asked… um, Ronnie? He was a senior, so it wasn't like she knew him well. "I live like a block that way, so I can get her to Terra Linda's hospital quickly."

"We'll have the office call her parents, Ron. That should be quick enough. Like I said, I'm not finding anything wrong with her," Coach Adams replied.

Alex and Bridget crowded in to see how she was doing. Bridget put her hand on her shoulder, while Alex said, "Hey, catch." She glared at the joke. "Not really funny, Alex."

He knelt down. "Maybe not. We'll look into it and make sure it doesn't happen again. Don't worry." It was a weird statement but oddly comforting. Alex was good at comforting and reassurance.

Angela and Bridget were working out by the creek, catching the little minnows in the stream. And whatever else wandered into their net. Bridget was controlling the net—she had the waders from helping her mom's research projects—while Angela had the camera. Bridget seemed to have a sixth sense as where the interesting catches were. Most of the minnows looked alike to Angela, but Bridget had identified steelhead and Coho salmon fry at a glance. "I'm telling you, Bridget, it was really weird the way they were going on. Alex said that someone named "Chiomara" had been talking to me, but I have no idea who that might be. I mean, what kind of name is that anyway?"

"Galatian." Bridget responded absently. "Well THIS doesn't belong here. Who was the idiot releasing gold fish into the creek?" She plopped the small fish into a bucket she'd brought along for that very purpose.

"Galatian? What on earth is Galatian?"

"Some Celtic tribes broke through the Greek city states, crossed into Anatolia—what we call Turkey—and settled down in the middle of the peninsula. They had their own province in the Roman Empire. For that matter the Christian Bible includes some letters to them from saint whatshisface."

"Paul?" she asked, amused.

"If you say so. I've never read it. Mom and Dad didn't see the point. They thought Aesop was better at morality lessons." Bridget was still speaking absently, paying a lot more attention to what she was doing with the net than the conversation she was having. "Ugh. Cans. Open up the recycle bag for me, would you?"

"Sure," she said, grabbing the white trash bag. The black one was for actual garbage. "But can you imagine secret names and stuff like that? I mean, what do you think they're up to? And how do you know the Galatian stuff"

"Well, since you ask, I *can* imagine secret names and stuff like that, and speculate on what they're up to. On the other hand," she said, standing straight up, net down in the water, and looking Angela directly in the eyes, "I don't need to imagine or speculate. I'm Chiomara, and Alex was an ass for letting you hear those names."

Angela barely held on to her notebook, as she stumbled on the rounded creek rocks. The anger radiating off Bridget was intense. But she'd just told Angela the truth. Bridget was, indeed, one of the people who were letting Seth off the hook and pressuring Alex to do the same.

"What do those names even MEAN?"

"Mean? Most of them don't mean anything. They're the names of our D & D characters. We wanted something private, something that would baffle anyone else, so we used those."

"He didn't mean any harm…"

"Intending harm isn't the POINT here, Angela. We had all agreed to keep them secret. We had agreed that no one else was to learn them until we were ready to have others know them. We had agreed that we could inform anyone we wished of our own names, but that we would not reveal the names of the others. That was the whole goal of the secrecy." She turned back to the creek, net working in the water. "And before you defend your would-be boyfriend some more, please, Angela, reflect a bit on how much you actually know about the matter." She was obviously still angry.

They continued working in the creek. Angela let Bridget cool off. "Bridget? Can I ask you something?"

She looked at her for a bit. "You can ask. I make no promise to answer."

Gulp. Bridget hadn't cooled down as much as she'd thought. "What happened at Halloween?"

"You had a sudden, intense, and fortuitous bout of diarrhea, that kept you safely out of the way while people who knew what they were doing dealt with a problem and didn't have to waste time and energy protecting an eager, brave, girl who lacked the knowledge and ability to protect herself in that situation. I know you like comparing things to movies. Think of how many protagonists basically get exceedingly lucky in surviving events. Then remember that this isn't a movie."

"Oh, come on, Bridget! What is so black ops that you can't tell me about it? I took down one of them…"

"And were taken down by the next." She held up a gloved hand. "You really don't need to know. I get that it's frustrating. But unlike Alex, I'm going to keep the secrets I've been entrusted with."

"Okay, okay. I'll stop asking." She held up both hands.

"Angela, I don't blame you for asking. It's perfectly natural that you're curious. I'm angry with Alex for not keeping the secrets. Do you have any idea how many arguments we've had? It really hasn't been at all pretty. It's been a stress on us we really don't need in addition to everything else we're keeping our eyes on. It's a good thing we're as nerdy as we are or we'd be having trouble in school, too. Alex could have handled it in a number of different ways, but he chose to do it in a way that betrayed us. The attacks on Seth had to stop. I don't know if he could have persuaded you to stop them on his own. But they need to stop."

"After what he did to me, you're surprised that my friends, my teammates, stepped forward and sought justice for me?" She said indignantly.

"You know as well as I do that the attacks weren't justified. Seth accepted a punishment from the COURT, Angela. He faced the justice system when he could have fought and won. Which doesn't even take into account what was really happening, that you don't understand even now. Angela, we haven't been entirely open with anyone, not just you. Only amongst ourselves. That's what the names signify to us. Alex essentially took it on himself to bring another into our little group, without consulting the rest of us, and it's a person—forgive me the description, but it is accurate—who is feuding with one of us over an event she does not understand, which deliberately or not she is using her faulty understanding of to cause harm to one of us, enough so that serious consequences are possible. We all should have had the opportunity to veto bringing anyone in."

Angela was starting to get angry herself . "Ok, hotshot, what DID happen? Because I was there. You weren't."

"Were you? Were you conscious the entire time? Were you aware of what happened? Well? As for what did… You've talked to Alex. You know perfectly well he was hurt and had a tree limb on top of him. He could only see so much. You haven't asked the only other person present, Angela. You've barely spoken to the only other person who knows what happened other than to accuse him of attacking you. Clear the air with Seth. Yeah, yeah, he lied to the principal. If you actually clear the air with him, you will learn why, and it will make sense." Bridget's hands were working and twisting around the handle of the net the whole time.

Angela bit her lip. She'd been unconscious. She knew that. She couldn't refute what Bridget had said, and her anger with Bridget evaporated. But Seth had still had his hand where it had no business being. She couldn't forget or forgive that. "I'm not talking to Seth, Bridget. The pervert was feeling me up."

"If you're not going to, that's your call, Angela. He's not going to approach you about it. He's far too shy around girls."

Angela and Carmen were headed to Spanish when they saw Alex and Dani. "Ange! Carmen! Alex was just suggesting we go to the initial Sirens-Avengers game on Sunday! Wanna come?" Dani called. She was wearing an Avengers t-shirt, purple with crossed lightning bolts.

"Seth's not going to be there, is he?"

Alex grinned. "No, he's in Sacramento. The Amazons are hosting the Valkyries. I suppose you could always ask Solomon to go with him."

"Yeah. San Jose has the bye, but it's Arcata versus San Diego, and Hollywood against Fresno," Dani put in.

"Are they…?"

"Well, Keisha drew the low card, you know. So she's staying home. But, yeah, the others will be with their teams."

"I thought it was all supposed to be secret hush hush."

He smiled. "Keisha's brilliance. The teams are set up as companies, in which we own all the stock, in trust for us for the next four years. But it's official—if not really public yet—that we're the owners."

"How did you manage that, Alex?" Carmen asked.

"You'd have to ask Keisha the money witch. She's the one who worked it so we could afford to do it."

"Well, then sure I'll come. Sounds great," Angela said, smiling.

Alex's box in Berkeley wasn't the most luxurious place to watch the game, but it had a good view, drinks on ice, snacks, and small screens covering the other three games. They were all being carried nationally on a start-up sports network and internet connection. The game was promising, and Angela started to imagine herself playing for one of these teams and catching the pass that capped a shut out season for the Valkyries. The receivers for both the Avengers and the Sirens were really good, repeatedly catching passes over the heads of the corners. She and Alex and Dani analyzed and dissected the game with all the fervency of the announce team… "I like the announcers. Where'd you find them?" Dani asked.

"They're locals. They're student callers for UC Berkeley. When they got offered actual jobs with us, they jumped at it. Malcolm has student callers from San Francisco State." Alex was speaking somewhat absently, his attention on the field. Like in Arcata, the Berkeley cheerleaders—called the Agents of Vengeance—were mostly guys. They weren't waving pom-poms, though. They'd fire a cannon, run banners down the sidelines, and pick up whoever scored for a "hip hip hooray" and carry her over to the sidelines. Malcolm's Triton Guards would do the same thing on his side of the field.

Around half time Angela left the room to go to the restroom; Alex was heading down to the locker room and Dani went with him. As she was headed down, she thought she saw someone shadowing her. When she emerged from the restroom, she again had that feeling of being watched and followed, and she got back to the box without anyone actually doing anything and without actually seeing anyone.

There was a call on the box phone while Alex was still down in the locker room. She glanced around a bit and decided to answer it. What harm could come from answering a phone? "Avengers Box!" she said.

A female voice answered. "Is Alex there?"

"No, he went down to the locker room with Dani. What's up?"

"Angela, this is Jennifer. Don't worry about it, I'll try his cell. League stuff."

"Okay. See you at school!"

"See you then!" they both hung up and Angela settled into the comfy, squishy chairs that Alex had equipped the room with. It seemed almost sinfully comfortable, and she was feeling a little tired.

"ANGELA! WAKE UP!" She gave a start and sputtered as ice water poured over her face and saw Dani leaning over her. She was somehow on the floor.

"You alright, Ange? You seemed to be sleeping like the dead, chica. It took that water to revive you. What was wrong?"

"Wrong? I dunno, I just sort of dozed off in that chair. It was so comfy and soft and I was feeling a bit sleepy."

"She looks okay to me, Alex. Probably nothing to worry about, so I'll get back over to my own box." She looked up and saw Malcolm. He smiled at her and left the room.

"I've got a trainer coming up to take a look at you, just to be on the safe side. You gave us something of a scare there Ange," Alex said. He did look worried. So did Dani.

"What was Malcolm doing over here?"

"He's been taking first aid training for as long as they let him in the classes, and he happened to be free and nearby." Well, his box was right next door. Since Alex and Malcolm were friends, that sort of placement really wasn't a problem. She supposed that it might be for another pair of owners, though.

About ten minutes passed before the trainer was able to come up and check her out. He couldn't find anything wrong with her, so he suggested making sure she wasn't alone and to have her doctor check her. So Alex and Dani stayed with her the rest of the day, watching the game, and Dani went with her to the restroom. It was a good rest of the day, and she enjoyed the time in the box.

A couple weeks passed uneventfully. She was pleased to note the Santa Cruz Valkyries were in last place, but the Avengers weren't doing so hot either; they'd won that game with the Sirens but lost the other two to the Starlets and the Sphinxes. Bridget's Unicorns were doing well, currently undefeated. Then Bridget brought up another trip in April—Monterey. San Francisco had a bye, but the Unicorns were playing the Valkyries on the other side of Monterey Bay. "Malcolm and I thought we'd dive in Monterey Bay on Saturday, catch the game on Sunday, and head back."

"I dunno, Bridget. My parents aren't going to like me down there with a boy." While ordinarily there would be a swim meet this weekend, half the Novato High team had come down with something, and a bunch of the others weren't feeling great. The County had called the meet off. So she and Malcolm were free.

"Oh, please? He's got something he wants to talk to Seth about, so he'll be in Seth's box for the game. Mom's not a football fan; you saw that up in Arcata. She'll be shopping in Carmel most of the day. But you can stay with us, Malcolm will be with his parents, we take their yacht out, and dive. You, um, can dive? Like scuba?"

"Yeah, I learned last summer so we could dive as a family off Okinawa."

"Fabulous!" Bridget beamed. "You've never gone into Monterey Bay? You're in for a fabulous time. Kelp forests, sea otters. You'll love it."

Malcolm's family's yacht was docked in Monterey; Angela had driven down with Bridget again. It seemed fast. It was big and roomy, with four bedrooms on board and plenty of room to store gear, and a little kitchen. She'd never really been around boats much in her life, so whatever gimmicks this one had were going over her head. She did have all her scuba gear, and getting up at four in the morning seemed a vile fate even if this should prove spectacular.

"OK, Angela, you'll be diving with the two of us," Malcolm said. He stood at the back of the yacht and was already geared up, ready to go. "If you get separated from us, surface. We'll find you. Dad will be staying aboard to keep an eye on things. Dr. Sullivan and Mom will be doing some diving of their own, with Mom as dive master. Okay?"

"Got it." She looked out over the waters of the bay, at the sea gulls above, the otters in the kelp. Then a huge shape surfaced and blew.

"Ah, a blue! Great. I wonder how close she'll come," Bridget said looking at the enormous whale.

"Close she'll come?" Angela asked, perplexed.

"Federal law, the Marine Mammal Protection Act, Angela, makes it illegal for us to disturb them. We don't approach them; if they want to come check us out that's different. Okay," Malcolm said. He pulled the coif of his wetsuit over his head and climbed down. "Bridget, you want to go first or do you want me to?" he asked.

"Why don't you go down first? That way I can help Angela if she needs it," Bridget responded. "No offense intended, Ange, but it sounds like you're the least experienced person here."

"Have you two been diving a lot?"

"At least once or twice a month for the past year," Bridget replied. "Up and down the coast, and last summer in the Mediterranean for me. Malcolm was nuts enough to dive in Antarctica over winter break."

"Which was awesome!" Malcolm called. "You should have been there!"

"Yeah, right, freezing my ass off in the middle of July. Not my favorite thing to do, Malcolm," Angela put in. He chuckled at her response, but then he adjusted his breathing apparatus and facemask and went in. She and Bridget did the same and soon they were diving down into the cold waters of Central California. They had lights on their gear, but the sunlight was streaming down. Malcolm was making rapid progress towards the sea floor, and Angela watched in amazement as a couple of dolphins swam right up to him. She looked over at Bridget and got an okay signal from her, and they dove down into the kelp forest, following Malcolm.

Sea lions and dolphins seemed to be cavorting all around them as they caught up to Malcolm, who was now doing a slow swim over the rocky bottom. He and Bridget were apparently engaged in some project; Bridget had a slate and stylus and Malcolm was using a camera. Angela wasn't quite sure what they were doing, but she was intent on having fun down here and seeing the sights. She swam away from where they were working, but kept them in sight, looking at the beautiful orange garibaldis and other fish she had no names for, the rock formations, the fuzzy sea otters that swam up and looked her over, the sharks swimming past and ignoring her. She wasn't paying much more attention to her surroundings than that when she suddenly felt the catch on her flipper.

She turned and it was someone in a bizarre costume. Black and green, with no obvious breather but fins and spines and sharp talons build into the gloves. The helmet even had a functional mouth with long sharp teeth like those of some sharks she'd seen at the museum. He—he didn't look like a woman in a wetsuit—reached out his taloned hands and ripped at her suit, scraping her skin on the arm and releasing blood. She kicked out and swam straight for Malcolm and Bridget with this freakazoid murderer in pursuit. She had to kick him away several times, but as she was approaching the other two, still absorbed in their task, he ripped away her hose. She screamed, with the strange effect that had under water. Malcolm and Bridget finally noticed what was happening to her as sharks started closing in.

Malcolm and Bridget swam straight for her. Malcolm pulled her away from the freak, put his own breather in her mouth, and bolted for the surface on smooth powerful strokes. Behind them the sharks were paying no attention to her; they'd all converged on the freak behind her... and tore him to pieces. They were in a feeding frenzy down there, and Bridget was still there! She tried to get Malcolm's attention, point out that Bridget was in danger, but he just kept pumping his flukes and pulsing his neck gills and… and… what the hell?

They burst the surface and she could see… his neck looked it's normal, muscular self. He was treading water. "Angela, you're bleeding and your equipment is trashed. Let's get you out of the water."

"Malcolm, Bridget's still down there in the middle of the sharks! We need to help her!"

"She's on her way back up, too. Don't worry about her. She can take care of herself, Angela." Malcolm was remarkably calm. "The sharks aren't going after her. They're just going after that poor guy."

"Malcolm, how the hell can you know that? Did you see those sharks?"

"I did, and they're following their instructions. Ah, here we go," he said as two huge black and white shapes surfaced beside them. "Try to avoid the blows." Something big and rubbery came up under her, with a tall black fin in front of her and Malcolm, and another killer whale surfaced with Bridget on it's back. She stared around.

"What the fuck is going on?"

Malcolm grinned at her. "I've been diving around here long enough that the local pods consider me a friend and come to my assistance. Don't worry about it, Angela." He considered her a bit longer. "Damn, but Seth was right about you. Let's get you onto the yacht."

"He usually is about this sort of thing, Malcolm," Bridget put in. "Let's get out of here. I got a sample of whatever that was. Malcolm, how clued are your parents?"

"About the same as yours, actually," he replied.

"That's good. So we won't have any trouble from that angle." Bridget was looking around, almost as if she could see through the water. "I think that was the only one."

The killer whales smoothly delivered them both to the yacht, but a sea fog rolled in. Angela was no weather expert, but she was pretty sure that this was an unusual… if not next to unnatural… occurrence. No one else could see them.

Malcolm's dad took charge. He got them cups of cocoa and the first aid kit. He applied betadine to the deep scratches and a gauze pad, then rolled more gauze over her arm. "Are you alright?" he asked her.

"She'll be fine, Dad."

"Yes, thank you, Mr. Muir," she said.

"Dr. Sullivan and Mom are still down there, Mal. Is there anything we need to be aware of?" he asked his son.

Malcolm shook his head. "They've got friends down there. I figured Bridget and I would be enough for our group, so I asked some friends to keep an ear on Dr. Sullivan and Mom. I think Seth was right, and it targeted Angela for some reason. Mom and Dr. Sullivan should be fine."

Angela was still a bit shocked from the whole thing, and she sipped her cocoa carefully. When they got back to shore, she intended to get some answers.

When they got back to shore, the grown ups went out for seafood and the three kids were sharing a pizza in Angela and Bridget's hotel room. Malcolm had actually wanted anchovies, but Bridget and Angela out voted him for sausage and onions. Angela finally burst out, "what did you mean, "Seth was right" about me? Right about WHAT about me?"

"Seth has a talent, you might call it, for guessing when someone will die and how, Angela. You mentioned to me that he'd correctly predicted your grandmother's death. As I recall you were certain that he'd done something to her. He hadn't. He can just tell.

"Back in August, he thought the bus accident was no such thing. He thought it was an attempt to kill you. And based on what we saw under the waves today, he was right," Malcolm said.

"That wasn't some guy in a suit, Angela. That was someone who had been deliberately altered to come after you, underwater. We don't know how, yet, or why, or by whom. But we're looking for the answers, I promise you. We aren't leaving you defenseless," Bridget said.

"What do you mean altered? Bridget, you're not making any sense here."

They looked at each other. Malcolm shrugged. "You know her better than I do. Can she handle it?"

Angela was stunned by the question he asked. "Handle what? Come on, guys, what is going on?"

"I think she can, yes. Somewhat, anyway," Bridget replied to Malcolm. He sat back and motioned, letting Bridget handle the conversation. He grabbed a slice of pizza.

Bridget looked at Angela, held out her hand, and said, "Fiat lux". A glowing green ball, the warm green of plants and growing things, appeared above her hand, floating there. Bridget took her hand away, and the ball of light continued to float in the middle of the room as Angela stared.

"The sharks were under my control, Angela. Malcolm would have had an easier job of it, but with your hose ripped we needed to get you to the surface. I've taken a look at the scrap of material I was able to get from them. That person had been human, once, but he'd been transformed by someone with out much knowledge. The DNA doesn't work as smoothly; he was essentially insane, simply following instructions. I think he could have actually survived, but something like that doesn't belong in the seas."

Malcolm put in, "I know you saw my transformation, even if you're trying to rationalize it. And yes. I had flukes and gills. I don't really NEED a wetsuit. It's protective camouflage in case we get seen."

"And as long as we're talking about it," Bridget said, reaching out and touching her arm, muttering something else Latin sounding, "There's no real reason to keep the bandage on any more." She took it off. Angela's skin was unmarred, completely. There was no evidence that she'd even been scratched. She looked at Bridget in wonder.

Malcolm looked at Bridget, and that feeling that some sort of communication had passed between them was even stronger. "You're noticing when we do that. We agreed not to talk about it, though. We've reached the limits of where we are going to speak. If you really want to know more, talk to Seth," Bridget said.

"As if!"

"We'll be in his box at the game tomorrow. I'm sure that you could walk over and talk to him if you wanted to," Malcolm said.

"Ah, Malcolm, he's not supposed to be within fifty feet of her," Bridget said.

"Right, so Skype is out? A phone call? A chat? A text? A tweet?" Malcolm sounded somewhat disgusted.

"I don't want anything to do with him! Bridget you can understand, cant you?" Angela said.

Malcolm threw up his hands in frustration. "Look, it doesn't give ME the bends. Talk to him, don't talk to him, I don't care. But the vote was unanimous. If you're ready to ask, it's Seth's duty and responsibility to tell."

"He's right, Ange. We can't discuss it. We promised. Telling our parents was our own responsibility, and I know one of us finds it more convenient to twist his parents' minds than tell them the truth. Mom knows in a general way. Malcolm's parents take advantage of it to dive in some of the remotest, most dangerous places in the world while knowing Malcolm can get them out. Everyone's different, Ange. A decision made in consensus can be returned to, but I don't think this one will."

"And why not? And how on God's green earth did I get saddled with Seth as my google search?" She said crossly.

Bridget's mouth quirked. "Well, both of those actually have the same answer. And it's one only Seth can give you. We promised." She looked over at Malcolm. "I'm less blasé about it than Malcolm is, but we're standing together on this. If you really want the answers, if you're ready to truly ask the questions and hear the truth, Seth is your man."

The rest of that evening the two of them steadfastly refused to answer Angela's questions about, well, magic and the supernatural. When she wanted to talk about something else they were more than happy to do that. It was incredibly frustrating to not be told the truth about what all was going on, and even worse to be thrown together with Seth. A few hours later Malcolm left and Dr. Sullivan returned to the room.

She tried to talk to Dr. Sullivan, too. Unfortunately, Dr. Sullivan didn't know much. Just like in the fall on the trip up to Arcata, she was polite, friendly, and pretty close-mouthed—or outright ignorant—about just about anything important. Like magic. Angela went to bed that night less than happy, to say the least. She didn't notice Bridget's green eyes gleaming in the darkness for a moment.

The next day Angela was in a much better mood. She didn't know why Malcolm and Bridget—and Alex and Teddy and Dawn, when she got back to school—weren't talking, but they had to have a good reason. They probably just wanted to heal over the potential problems she'd been posing, when she over heard them and their strange names in the grove of oaks. That made the most sense. If they could get her and Seth back to normal speaking terms, their problems among themselves would be overall solved. Certainly that's what Teddy had made it sound like. Elements from earlier in the year were starting to fall into place. If they had magic, they used it to investigate the cheerleaders' murders and catch the guy. She wouldn't really NEED to talk to Seth at all, just keep her eyes and ears open so she knew what was happening. And it's not like Reverend Johnson's inflamed three in the morning Sunday public access show, screaming about black magic and the evils of Harry Potter and Dungeons and Dragons and all that were anything anyone paid attention to. Realizing all that made her a lot happier.

The game was great. She dropped asking the questions that she knew perfectly well that Bridget wasn't going to answer. She and Bridget mostly had the box to themselves, cheering the passes and Unicorn scores and big plays. She loudly booed the successes by the Valkyries' offense, even when Jessie Blaylock, who used to go to LVH, scored; Bridget and Alex didn't have anyone that young on their teams. Bridget even joined in once or twice, but she was mostly sitting back and cheering her own team when they made a stop rather than the Valkyries' mistakes. An old Jane Austen movie also playing had them in fits. A knock at the door let in Malcolm in a Sirens jersey, after they'd turned the laptop off.

"Thought I'd come over here and see how you girls were getting along."

They looked at each other and giggled. Bridget came out of it first. "Ah, we're, ah, fine, Malcolm." She looked back over at Angela, and they both started giggling again. This time Angela recovered first.

"Whyever do you ask, my good fellow?" she said. 'Why, we're the best of friends! The absolute best!"

"I didn't know your Mom brought along her rum supply, or that you'd been sipping the fairie wine," he replied.

"Now now, Malcolm, let's dance. Come on now, put your feet like so… and like so…" He gave off a very high pitched squeal that had them both grabbing their ears instead of him. Then he looked at both of them glaring at him, and handed a paper to Angela with a series of numbers on it.

"Angela, Seth's contact information, should you wish to pursue an inquiry into the world we've come to inhabit."

"Um, gee, thanks?"

"Now, if you're interested in a little scuttlebutt I picked up over with Seth," he raised his eyebrows at them expectantly. They looked at each other still rubbing their ears from that shriek.

"Ok, Malcolm. If it's good, we're even for that shriek of yours. How do you do that anyway?"

"I imitate the dolphin. But onto the scuttlebutt! It seems that Molly Webb is pregnant," he said, naming the head quarterback of the Sacramento Amazons. Bridget's mouth fell open, although Angela couldn't see the surprise or the humor.

"Really? Molly Webb?" Angela asked.

"The one and only Molly Webb."

"Does she have to go on leave or something?" Angela asked.

"Keisha and Solomon drew up the league rules on that, so I'm not entirely sure." He looked at Angela's confused expression. "Solomon's parents are obstetricians. We wanted to make sure all were safe."

"Solomon, you idiot," Bridget burst out with laughter.

"Huh? He's not the dad is he? He's our age!" Angela exclaimed.

"It's not biologically impossible, Ange," Bridget replied. "And unfortunately, Solomon's extremely talented at inducing pregnancy, or at least fertilization. Last time he dove with us, he increased the fertility rates of just about everything down there with only a little concentration. He really enhanced the ecosystem."

"So, yeah, it's a good bet, really, that the kid is his. I'm not sure that she'll ever admit to it, of course; there are laws against sleeping with your underage boss, you know. But if you ever find yourself in a position to date Solly, I suggest you don't unless you want to have a baby."

"Okay, creepy! I'm going to go get some wings. You guys want anything?" Angela said grabbing her purse.

"Ah, no thanks."

"None for me, thanks," said Malcolm, somewhat dreamily. His eyes were closed. "The wings booth over here has a long line and is almost out. Try the other side. They've been hit hard for nachos, but have plenty of wings."

"Gee, thanks!" She headed out and that way. There were plenty of people visiting the concession stands as she walked around the stadium. She spotted what looked like a short cut and slipped into the back way. Then she was alone; not even workers were around as she trotted through the darkened storage area at least seventy feet across. And that was when the attack came.

A dart impacted above her head, and her winged attacker worked a bolt. It was a trank gun, but he was in the air, just hovering, on great-feathered wings. It didn't look possible for them to be holding him up, but they were. He fired again, and another dart barely missed. The room got suddenly even darker, and she darted herself towards the exit while he was reloading and slipped. As she was scrambling to get out of the line of fire she heard a thump. Her attacker lay unmoving, fallen from the air. Seth appeared in the darkened area, well away from Angela, nodded to her, and bent over her attacker. He was wearing a black suit, complete with black shirt and tie. He didn't even ask how she was. What a jerk! She got to her feet and kept going to the concession stand.

When she looked back, Seth and the attacker were both gone. She got her wings and made her way back to the box, this time keeping to the main corridors even if they were a little crowded; it was better than running into another attacker, or, worse, Seth. When she got back to the box, it was empty. Bridget and Malcolm were gone. Then she heard Bridget's voice.

"Angela. Sorry we're not here, but Seth just killed one of your attackers. He got some information out of him, though. We're over in Seth's box. Seth said you were fine. I've got some alarms and such up around the box that will go off if anyone unauthorized tries to get in. Seth wants to know what you thought you were doing wandering around in a maintenance area, but that's not really important." The voice had spoken from nothingness, just started talking with no real source. That was creepy. Just like Seth. She settled down in one of the comfy chairs to watch the game.

About half an hour later the door opened. Angela scrambled out of her chair and picked up a souvenir football, ready to hurl it with all her strength at whoever was coming in, but it was Bridget. Angela relaxed. "What happened over there?"

"It looks like who we thought was behind it really was," Bridget replied. "Unfortunately, it's nothing we can actually report to the cops and let them handle."

"What do you mean? You said you got some information out of him before he died right?"

Bridget looked at her. "Angela, first, did you see what attacked you? I guarantee you all the questions are going to be asked about what that was, not on anything important. Second, *I* didn't get the information, Seth did. And Seth's method of information gathering isn't going to impress the cops or be believed by a judge." At Angela's expression, she sighed. "Seth pulled memories out of his dead brain, Angela. I don't even know how he does it."

"Oh. Oh, yeah, they wouldn't believe that. Damn. So what's happening?"

"Well, while we were over there we got a call from Alex. He just foiled an attack on Dani. We're going to need to do something about it, but we're still trying to find something that would let the cops pull a raid on the place the bad guys are holed up. There are… innocents in the way, if we tried to go after them ourselves." She paused. "And there are some other issues."

C H A P T E R

The Team Hike was… an unusual thing, but Coach Nguyen seemed to think recreating together would help bring them together as a team, during the off-season for football. The older kids seemed to look forward to it every April. Dani of course wasn't along, as she was still nursing her ankle after that softball game, and there were a few boys nursing their own injuries or with parents who had something else for them to do. Coach had them in a buddy system, and Angela got Alex. She got a little nervous as he came over. They smiled at each other a little nervously. "Hey Ange. Good to see you again. How's it been in Bioland?" her asked. He was wearing an Avengers windbreaker and baseball cap over his shirt and shorts

"Ok. I'm passing the class, at least, thanks to Bridget," she replied.

"I think you'd have at least something to do with it. She's not taking the tests for you."

"Ready for the hike, then?" she asked.

"Absolutely."

The hills they were hiking were the bright green of winter mixed with the brown and gold of summer and autumn. The fire roads weren't exactly mud, but they were still dirt rather than dust. The chirping of birds helped make the hike an inspiration. Angela raised her face to the sun and drank in the warmth.

"You know, Ange, I'm glad you and I got named hiking buddies," he said.

"Oh?" she asked, her heart fluttering a bit. "Why's that?"

"I forgot my canteen and such. But now that we're away from everyone else, your trip down to Monterey means I don't need to worry about you seeing this." He picked up a fairly large stone and stared at it for a bit. In a few seconds it had become a normal canteen with a strap. He took the cap off and visibly poured water into his mouth. "Drink?" he asked with a smile on his face.

She blinked rapidly at him. This was something she hadn't anticipated even when she'd learned about it from Bridget. Other than the emergency of getting her to the surface, neither Bridget nor Malcolm—nor anyone else—had actually used their powers in such a blatant way in front of her. Granted she hadn't seen much of Alex, now that football season was over and she was concentrating on volleyball and swimming, but she'd been catching glimpses of all the people she thought had the powers. She wasn't sure who all did what, or precisely why they were doing it.

'They were hiking down a deer trail on the far side of the hill when they heard the roar from a clump of trees. It was... a feather covered dinosaur-thing, at least twenty feet tall, and even longer with the massive tail. The head of a crocodile roaring on a long thick neck, with a mane of feathers surrounding the head. Long powerful arms, nothing at all like a T-rex, equally covered in feathers but with three long claws stretching from each hand. The back legs looked like they was solid muscle and larger in diameter than her waist. Blood dripped from feathers and talons and fangs. Angela ran.

Alex looked about and called to her, "I am really glad that Bridget and Malcolm talked to you already. That means this isn't going to shock you."

"What isn't?" she asked, barely comprehending the thing out of a nightmare. It roared again and darted towards her.

With a few words—she couldn't make them out—and a finger coming down, a massive lightning bolt came out of the slightly cloudy sky to impact directly on the thing. The lightning bolt blinded her, the thunder picked her up and she tripped. Then she heard it roar again, felt Alex's hands picking her up. A surge of energy went through her and she could see again; the pain that had started in her knees and palms vanished. She was fine, but the thing was coming straight at them. The air seemed to chill around them as Alex invoked some other gibberish and surrounded its' feet with ice.

It slowed the monster a little. Then it burst free of the ice and continued to dart towards them like some sort of monstrous bird. It's jaws closed on Alex, only to confront a gleaming purple shield and be thrown back the distance of the football field. But getting up it was obvious the thing was unhurt.

"At least I don't have to hide this from you! Damn, that would be a pain!" He said as he hurled another bolt of electricity, this time from his hand.

"What about fire? I thought you people liked fire!"

"Are you kidding? Bridget would have my ass if I started a grass fire up here!" he responded, tossing another electric discharge at it as it came forward again. "Ange, get moving!" He nodded at her and she felt her legs moving faster. Angela used her newfound speed to dodge around the thing, trying to split its' attention. It charged towards her until Alex hit it with another blast of frigidly cold air and slowed it's reactions down. Then it roared and returned its' attention to Alex. Alex vanished in a flash of purple light to reappear by Angela's side.

The thing, enormous, covered in bloody feathers, jagged teeth dripping with more, nostrils flaring stalked towards them on massive feet. "Run, Ange!" He motioned with his hands and a bolt of electricity struck the creature. It staggered briefly, but mostly seemed to ignore the blast.

"Where to, Alex?!" The hike was a nightmare as the thing approached. It bellowed anger at Alex and kept coming. "I don't suppose you can just get us out of here?"

"I've never tried bringing someone with me, Ange! And these aren't doing much!" he responded.

"Can you whistle up some help, then?"

"I can, but you won't like it," he replied grimly. A rock lifted off the ground and smashed into the creature's head. That got its attention but it still kept coming towards them. They were down off the hill now and moving faster than they should be able to. "Shit that thing's skull is hard. What'd they make it out of?"

Angela found a rock of her own and beaned the thing with it. 'Whaddya know? Softball pitching's good for something! And what do you mean I won't like it?" She asked as she found another rock to throw just as Alex tried a blast of fire.

"Who do you think I can call on?" The sweat was pouring off him now as the creature dowsed the flames in its feathers.

"What about Dawn?"

"She's in Seattle with her older brother looking at colleges." Another clap of thunder shook the thing.

"Bridget?"

"San Diego, with Jenny." Lightning hit the creature again.

"What about Malcolm?" she asked, throwing fast and hard.

"Cabo San Lucas. And underwater, most likely. And Teddy's at a church retreat with his parents, Solomon's in Arizona, and Keisha's visiting New Orleans,"

"I thought those weren't working well! Who does that leave?"

"They aren't, but they're easier for me than something else. Seth! Angela and I are in the hills, and we need your help." His voice took on an odd note, almost prayerful,

"Seth? You're calling on Seth for help?"

"He's at home and available." He paused to grow a massive hand out of the ground to grab a hold of the monster. It slowed the creature a bit, before it tore loose and kept coming. Alex snapped off another lightning bolt and a tree reached out to grab the monster. It held it briefly but again the monster tore threw it. "He wants to know if you'll accept his assistance or if you're going to go berserk at his mere presence."

"Berserk?!" Angela was furious even as she kept throwing rocks… and the occasional solid dirt clod—at the creature.

"His word, not mine," came Alex's response as he sent yet another blast of electricity at the monster. He was starting to look tired.

"Oh, alright. Let him come." She was tired, her legs were aching from the hike and the running from the monster. Worse, she was running out of rocks. Maybe the perve could help. If not that beast was going to eat them.

"Seth, we entreat your aid." A flash of light, a pop of air, and Seth was floating in the air nearby. He was wearing the usual black shirt and pants and shoes, but he also wore a cowled black robe—a silk robe—over them.

There were a few decorations on the hem of the robe in bone-white thread that Angela couldn't make out well.

"Did you analyze it?" he said calmly as the air around them took on a dark tint. His robe billowed out around him. The creature paused briefly, noting the new arrival.

"No, not yet. Been a little busy keeping us alive, you know," Alex responded, much more his calm, cheery self.

Angela threw another rock, only for it to rebound in mid air. "The defense will let energy through, and small molecules, but not something that large. At least not for now, but it can take only so much before it collapses, Miss Fujimori. Please do not inflict additional damage on the barrier protecting us," Seth said. He turned his attention back to Alex. "How do you plan on defeating it if you don't analyze it, Alex? It's not like you to be so dense." Seth's calm was creepy. It was as if he didn't even consider the thing coming towards them a threat. Alex was muttering something and his eyes glowed purple. He stared at the creature as it smashed into Seth's barrier again and again.

"Can't you create a solid barrier? Impenetrable?" she asked Seth, who's attention seemed focused on the defense. He glanced at her.

"Well, yes, of course. But an absolutely solid impenetrable barrier would also be impenetrable to things like oxygen and carbon dioxide. Which would be bad, you know."

Then Alex turned those glowing purple eyes on Seth. "Oh, you bastard. REALLY?! Nothing conductive at ALL? The bolts were just doing pinpoint burns?" Seth blandly smiled at him. "Rubberized skin? Plasticized teeth and claws? How did you swing that, Seth? I get the Aztec monster theme, and thank you for the heritage boost, but really!"

"I asked Bridget for a little help. I still remember the animate rock monster you helped Keisha with," Seth replied, looking quite smug. "Payback's a bitch."

"You have too easy a time with anything dead. And it's almost as bad with anything living," Alex retorted. "If we don't do something animate like that, it's not even a challenge for you."

"Mmmm. You might have a point. What are you going to do about this thing, anyway?" Seth inquired, eyebrows raised

"WHAT ARE YOU TWO TALKING ABOUT? Alex, did Seth make this thing and send it after us?"

Seth answered before Alex could. "Don't be ridiculous. I didn't send it after you. I didn't even know you'd be here. I sent it after ALEX. It's a test of his abilities."

"You didn't? C'mon, Seth." Alex asked. "You knew this was the team hike."

"Team hike, yes, I knew that. That Angela would be your hiking buddy, no. I was expecting Mike van Ledder," he said, naming the center, "to tell you the truth. Do you still have the energy to finish it?"

"Yeah, I think so. Can you get Angela out of here? I know you've pulled Cerberus and Orcinus and Macaria with you at different times," Alex said, looking back at the creature. He squinted, and took a stick. Within seconds it had morphed itself into a handle, and a thrumming purple blade came out. "This more like what you were expecting?"

"To answer the second question first... precisely how you win is up to you. There are multiple strategies that will work. Whether or not your chosen strategy will work... we'll see.

"As for getting Angela out..." He pressed his lips together.

"She's part of the test, isn't she? Defense of another?" Seth inclined his head, but didn't say anything. Their discussion of her while not talking to her was infuriating.

"I'm right HERE you two! And I'm not going anywhere! Can you make me one of those?"

"She seems to have decided to stay, so no I won't be getting her out. And no comment."

"Ok, Angela, sure. Get me a stick, would you?" She went looking, but could still over hear the soft voices of the boys thinking her out of range.

"Thantoris, really, get her out of here. This is a test of me, she's an innocent. Get her out of here, please."

"Toranos, old boy, she doesn't want to go. If you fail the test, I'll deal with the thing."

"HEY! Are you saying you can destroy that thing here and now and we can go for ice cream?" Angela demanded. She handed Alex a stick.

Alex looked at her. "Of course he can. He made it. You're forgetting this is a test? What'd you use, anyway?" He handed her back a handle.

The blade that snapped out when she pushed the button was black. Alex and Seth traded a look.

"Not until after the test is over, Alex."

Angela stared at the black energy blade in her hand. "What the?"

"Do you have a favorite color, Angela?" Seth asked.

"Yeah, teal, why?"

"Hmm. Never mind." From the looks on their faces, it wasn't a "never mind", but Bridget and Malcolm had been almost as silent on things.

"Look, I know from Bridget and Malcolm that you guys are Harry Potter wizards. For that matter I've just been watching it running for our lives from the monster. What the hell does black on my light saber mean? Or is that part of the test, too?"

"This isn't a test of you, Angela, it's a test of ME," Alex replied. "Did I just lose points?"

"It's odd, Alex, I'll give you that," Seth said. He rubbed his head, running his hand through his hair. "Have you ever made one for someone else? Someone other than one of us, I mean?" He gestured at a handle at his own waist. Seth did fencing?

Alex contemplated that for a moment. "Not something real. I made some fakes for my cousins, but those were the plastic variety."

"Maybe that accounts for it."

"I guess," he replied. "I don't really know."

"We should probably look into it once this is over," Seth said. "And speaking of which?"

"Yes, yes. Drop the barrier any…" The dark tint to the world was gone, and the monster charged straight at Angela. Alex leaped forward to intercept it and sliced off the tip of its snout, enraging the thing but prompting it to take a step back and reassess. It roared again and came in with arms splayed wide, one aimed toward Alex and one towards Angela. Angela dodged around to the side and stuck her blade in. As it roared and snapped at her Alex put another slice through its hand and removing two of the clawed fingers. It screamed and turned back towards him. Angela swung at its leg, carving off a good sized dark brown slice and barely danced out of the way of a clawed foot. Alex, slicing away at the stomach of the monster, dropping several pale pieces of the monster, was grabbed by one of the claws even as Angela lopped off the tip of the tail.

Seth…sat there in a darkened bubble and did nothing as the creature's maw came down upon Alex's head. A burst of purple beams erupted from Alex, shredding the clawed hand, the head, and the body just as a nearly panicking Angela sliced its leg off.

"So what was that thing?" Angela asked as they looked over its smoking corpse. It stank of burned rubber, but they'd chopped it to pieces with high temperature light sabers. It still twitched, as if trying to move and attack

"Roadkill turkey," Seth responded. "Goodbye, Pandora." The monster stopped it's twitching and dissolved into exactly what Seth had called it—a turkey. One of the many that wandered the hills around Lucas Valley. Smashed up almost beyond recognition, without a head or tail or wing or leg, but a turkey.

"Pandora? Really? SETH!" Alex exploded laughing. "Are you telling me all I had to do was greet it by NAME to destroy it?"

"How were you supposed to know THAT?" Angela demanded.

"Seth's idea of a joke, actually." Alex kept laughing, and wiped his eyes. "Did you ever read "Frankenstein"?"

"Um, no…"

"In the book, 'Frankenstein' was the name of the doctor. The name of the *monster* was Adam." He looked expectantly at her.

She was still confused. "I don't get it."

"This thing," he nodded at it, "was Seth's version of Frankenstein's monster, but he built it from a female turkey. He doesn't think much of Abrahamic myth, but does find Greek and Norse and Egyptian interesting. So… he named it after the first woman in Greek mythology. Which was Pandora."

"Greeting her by name was the extra credit portion of the test. There's almost always a way to pass the test without using violence." Angela and Alex watched as Seth pulled a small amphora from the bird's chest cavity. "In the original myths," he explained, "Pandora had a jar, not a box. If you'd been paying attention, you'd have noticed the jar and known to hit it. You kept using electricity and frigidity and finally, high temperature lasers, to chop it to pieces. With the exception of that rock and Angela's contribution, you didn't try simple force and accuracy, and Angela didn't know to aim for it." He looked over at her. "Brave of you to stand and fight."

"You nearly killed us!"

He rolled his eyes. "Great. This again. Alex, see you tomorrow. I'm outta here." He spoke some gibberish and vanished.

"You know, Ange, this was aimed at me. There's no reason to be mad at Seth."

"He could have waited to unleash that thing until you were with one of the others."

"Other what? Other nine? Like, say, Bridget or Teddy? Wouldn't have worked. The idea was that I needed to protect someone, someone who doesn't have the abilities and power that I do."

"Hey, I helped!" Angela protested. "I was not some stupid princess who couldn't defend myself waiting for big strong man to come save me!"

"I never said you were, and neither did Seth, if you were paying attention. You jumped in to help. I might not have passed the test without your assistance. On your own, rocks. With my help, a crazy sword. I'm guessing ultraviolet, which is why it appeared black. But I don't really know." Alex said. "I'm not sure how they're going to count that."

"Speaking of which, what was the big deal about the saber being black, anyway?" she asked him, hoping he'd actually talk to her.

"Well. I happen to like purple. When I made them for the other nine—yes, Seth has one, even if you never see it—they came out in their favorite colors. Bridget's is green. Keisha's is orange. Jenny's is indigo. Teddy's is red."

"And Seth's?" She had a premonition of what color Seth's was.

"Black," he said flatly. "I'm not sure why yours came out black. I'd have expected purple, as I made it, or teal, as your color. I'll look into it and get back to you."

"Get away from me! You now you're not supposed to be this close to me!" Angela shouted as Seth passed by their table.

"This is the school library, and you came in half an hour after I did. I can't exactly use the exit without passing by you since you can't seem to set foot farther than the first table inside the doors. I'm not stalking you. I'm not sneaking around looking for a date. I don't even like you very much. And I'm leaving now," he replied. "Hello, Bridget," he said as he walked out the doors. The worst part was he could probably use the sunshine.

Bridget looked at Angela quizzically. "I know he's never been your favorite person, Ange, but really, what's your problem with Seth NOW? It's not like he's ever made a habit of coming near you." Her pencil kept scratching away at the assignment.

"He almost got me killed this weekend!"

"What? How?"

"He made that feathered dinosaur thing and sent it after us?"

"Feathered dinosaur?" Bridget asked quizzically.

"Yeah! He even claimed you helped with it!"

"Oh," she chuckled. "Alex's test, you mean? That WAS inspired, wasn't it? The whole concept was fabulous." She caught Angela's disbelieving glare "I know how it must have looked, Ange, but honestly, you were in no danger at all." She shook her head. "None at all. And if Alex had kept his head he'd have realized it, too."

"What do you mean?"

"Alex's test involved protecting an innocent. Seth passed with flying colors last month, and DAMN did he do it quickly. He knocked him out for fifteen minutes and made him incorporeal for ten. Only Jenny did it faster, simply teleported her home. But anyway, Alex could have given you flight and gotten you out of the way, or some sort of super speed. Or if he'd meta'd the test he might have realized Seth had taken a page from Teddy's book and just made it look like you were being threatened." She paused and leaned forward at Angela's disbelieving expression. "I was there when he programmed the turkey. It was set to go after Alex and only Alex, but to feint a few times in the direction of any others around or take down any erected barriers. YOU were fine."

"I don't trust the perve. How do you know he didn't change its instructions once he knew it was me there?"

"I don't know that. Other than to say it wouldn't be like Seth to do that." She cocked her head.

"Could he have kept direct control?" Angela demanded. Just because he programmed the thing, didn't mean he couldn't have given it other instructions.

"Yes. Yes, he could have. I don't think that he has that sort of animosity towards you, though. In fact, I'm sure he doesn't."

"Ha. Well, then, can we stop talking about the pervert and talk about biology?"

"Sure." She glanced over at Angela's worksheet. "Especially since your mind appears to have been somewhere completely different than school. The definition of ecology is not "I'm in love with Death." And I've never seen any diagram of a cladistic tree built around that stylized skull."

Angela looked down at her paper. There were repeated references to death—most of them romantic—and that skull appeared all over the page. She grabbed her eraser. "Oh, why won't Mrs. Kravitz let us do this on a computer?"

"Because it's too easy to cheat. Besides, you did that absent-mindedly. What were you thinking anyway?"

"I don't know. Isn't it bad enough he groped me? He has to be messing with my head, too?"

Bridget looked at her pensively. "That's not exactly his style, though. And you're wearing that really cute pink and white outfit. I think if Seth were messing with your mind, you'd be in black. Leather."

Angela glared at her, only to realize she was being teased as Bridget grinned at her. "Very funny."

"It really isn't his style," she said, narrowing her eyes. "You've got something…" her voice got a bit distant, "If you'll permit me?" She stretched out her hand towards Angela's head,

"Permit you to do what, Bridget?"

"Examine your mind to determine if someone has tampered with you. You have my word that I will do nothing to alter or influence your mind without your permission."

Angela blinked at her. Yes, Bridget was one of the nine, but… "You think someone did something?"

"Maybe. May I examine you? Skin contact makes it a lot easier for me, so I'd like to be touching your head while I do this."

That didn't really make any sense to Angela, but if Seth had tampered with her mind… "Yes, please Bridget."

"Okay." She rested her fingertips across Angela's face and closed her eyes. They sat there for almost a minute. Angela could tell Bridget was doing something, as she almost felt the gentle probes as pressure applied inside her skull and various memories scampered to the surface. She colored slightly at all the memories of Alex. Then Bridget jerked back into her own seat. She shivered as Bridget spoke. "Well, well, well."

"What?" Angela demanded.

"I think you're OK."

"What are you talking about? Of course I'm OK. He's the…" Bridget wasn't paying attention to her, eyes glazed over as she stared into space.

"Oh, my goodness."

"What? Bridget, you're being even stranger than normal. What the hell are you talking about?" Bridget had returned to the present, at least.

"OK, sorry, Angela. Someone was influencing your mind. And someone else stopped it." She paused. "Ah, I should have guessed. One thing about Seth, he's patient. If he likes you, and I'm not saying he does,

I don't know one way or the other, he'll patiently wait for you to come to him, not make you put that on your homework."

"What do you mean? He's the one who was in my head wasn't he?"

Bridget gave her a crooked smile. "Yes, yes he was in your head. It's just… I'm completely certain he's the one that stopped the tampering and put in that tripwire I found when I took a look. I'm just glad it was keyed to the person who was doing the tampering and not just anyone."

"Who was messing with my mind, then?" she challenged. Bridget shook her head.

"I'd rather not say just now, Angela. I want to confirm it before I accuse someone. Seth just challenged me when I probed your mind, which is why I'm sure he was the one who stopped it. But… Angela, Seth is very dangerous, and he's actively defending you. You might want to think about that next time you're going to rant about what he did last August." She kept writing for a few moments, then locked eyes with her. "And by "very dangerous", I mean that if Seth Dupree wanted you dead, you would be, and nothing, and I mean *nothing*, I or Alex or anyone else could do would prevent it."

The ride out to the theater wasn't that scenic, but since it was out Lucas Valley Road towards the bay it was mostly flat. Angela was looking forward to meeting Karen, Carmen, Joy, and Liz for the matinee. She was glad she was still wearing her sunglasses; the sun seemed exceptionally bright out here. There was almost a flash; something reflected the light so much it looked like a flash while Angela was standing in the snack line waiting for her nachos and sprite. A few minutes later they saw Dawn Takugawa walk in with Juan Lopez, Shirley Takeshita, and Solomon Levison. The guys seemed to be putting on brave faces, so presumably the girls had picked the movie.

Angela and her friends were going to "Soothe the Savage Beast" in 3d, billed as a rom-com version of "Beauty and the Beast". What they needed the blue and red glasses for they didn't know, but were eager to find out. They got their snacks, popped on the 3d shades, and took their seats. The movie was great. The movie had been made on budget, with new actors, but the guys were hunky and the girls smart. Some of the scenes almost looked like they were going to spill out into the audience, the 3d was so real—the exceptionally violent scenes, the crashing down of the tower, the rage of the beast, the sweeping fire seemed so hot… but it was just a … a … movie.

As she and her friends got up to leave, she spotted Dawn and Solomon in the back of the theater with their dates. Although the air conditioner had seemed to come back on and restore the chill air of the normal theater, Dawn and Solomon were both sweating heavily. As they left, they both nodded to her, in acknowledgment of her presence… and she nodded back, mouthing "thank you", knowing that they hadn't been here to watch a movie, but to keep it from becoming a conflagration. She shivered a little, almost as if she passed under an air vent, at how close that had come to being a disaster.

At school the next Monday she tracked down both of them to say the "thank you" out loud. They had a geometry class together, and that was where she found them.

"Not a problem, Angela," Dawn replied, smiling. Her smile made her face radiant, as if a cloud had stopped blocking the sun. She glanced at Solomon. "But you should know, in most of these instances, even if we're the ones actually present, we're not exactly the ones you need to be thanking."

"Not that the thanks are unappreciated, you understand," Solomon said smiling at her himself. The dark haired boy seemed to be looking right past her until Dawn's hand whacked his shoulder. "She's right, though. We were the ones who happened to be free to go see that movie. They could have greatly improved it by…" thwack "… We were sent, actually."

Angela looked down uncomfortably at the ground. This was making altogether too much sense. "By Seth, right? You were sent to stop that by Seth?" She swallowed audibly while she waited for what she knew would be the answer.

"Yes," Dawn said quietly. "He identified the next attack as coming at the theater that day. And the bad guys are getting better at concealing their intentions, too. He barely had the time to get the information to us." Dawn was looking decidedly on the grim side, almost like the sun through smoke.

"So what happened?" Angela asked.

"The bad guys got their hands on the copy of the movie sent to this theater. They altered it in a few key places, to where it could become deadly if triggered. I think they had a person of their own in the audience providing the triggering mechanism," Solomon responded. "Probably a girl, although they haven't used one since Sarah Campbell. Whoever it was, it was a suicide mission; they'd never have survived the conflagration if they'd succeeded. They really could have improved the movie if they'd just…" thwack. "Enough already!"

"Solly, I've been hearing your ideas for improving that movie ever since you first saw a trailer for it. Since we saw the Disney version way back when! Not interested in hearing it again! Neither is Bridget, nor Jennifer, nor Keisha! I do not think for one iota of time that Angela's at all interested!"

"Well, if you're going to be that way about it," he huffed, the picture of wounded dignity. Angela didn't really believe his act. Dawn snorted at his antics. He obviously didn't take it seriously.

"That brings me to a point I wanted to discuss with you," he said. "Have you and Bridget ever discussed protective jewelry?" His eyebrows were raised.

"Jewelry can be protective?" She asked, puzzled.

"Oh, yes, yes indeed. Provided one of us has worked with it. As it happens, we've been considered some means of giving you some passive defense, just in case. Would you be amenable to that?"

"Have you figured out why I'm being targeted yet?" She asked in response.

"No, I'm afraid nothing we've come up with makes any sense for someone to be repeatedly targeting you with these sorts of powers in some kind of death curse," Dawn replied.

"There is that one idea of Teddy's. You know the one, Dawn."

"What, that it doesn't make any rational sense because the motives of the attacker don't make any rational sense? That he's…"

"Gone insane with the passage of time," Solomon said, nodding.

"What do you mean?"

"We agree—that is, Seth, Bridget, and I agree—that our adversary has used his abilities to extend his life beyond normal limits. We haven't figured out how he did it yet, but he's basically been walking around—and concealing his true identity—for centuries. That's getting increasingly difficult to do, according to most of what we've read, just with modern technology"

"Why is there so much time between some attacks and not others?" Angela asked

"That's more a question for Jennifer." Dawn replied, "But basically it's a matter of preparing the weapon or tool. He's shown a preference for altering someone to fulfill the role of assassin rather than coming himself or relying on... oh, Jenny and Seth can just be unhappy... spells from afar. The two in Santa Cruz, you know? It takes time to turn someone or something into a homing killing weapon."

"Or to control their minds so thoroughly that they'll so whatever you want whenever you want to whoever you want," Solomon put in.

"We'll get him one way or another, Angela. Don't worry."

The Spring Formal was the school dance for the younger students, as opposed to the Prom. Angela had gotten asked by Solomon Levison, but despite him being one of the nine, Angela had politely turned him down, after that conversation in Santa Cruz. She didn't want a baby. She also was looking for a date to the dance, not a bodyguard. She had accepted the invitation of Marcus Newton, a pitcher on the baseball team. All these athletes at dances and she'd never quite been satisfied. Ugh. Could the person messing with her mind be right? Could she really have a deep seated, unacknowledged longing for Seth? How horrible a thought! She must not have kept that off her face very well, because Marcus asked what was wrong.

"Oh, nothing, nothing at all," she lied to him, smiling. She didn't think he believed her, but he didn't press. He just nodded and went off to get her a Sprite. Wasn't a sprite a kind of faerie? All this magic stuff going off around her! It was driving her batty. At least she could come to the dance, do something normal without worrying about it. All the same, she was happy to see the eight normal members of the nine present and dancing. Solomon had ended up asking her friend Joy. She wanted to warn Joy about him, but couldn't figure out the words to do it. Solomon was nice, smart, funny. There was nothing objectively wrong with him,

She and Marcus got out on the dance floor. She stayed on the floor for quite a while, as her JV teammates wanted to dance with her, and she noticed that Carmen was here with Teddy and Karen was here with Malcolm. Keisha was here with Mike Wu, of course; Keisha and Mike had become a well known couple. Bridget had come with Patrick O'Brien, of the offensive line. Jennifer was present with Michael Erlingson and she spotted Dawn with Julian Kanekawa. Then Teddy grabbed her for a dance... a slow dance. She thought about refusing after all the teasing, but maybe this was more than it seemed, so she accepted and they started dancing.

"Be watchful, Angela," Teddy said as they danced. "Seth passes warning. There will be another attempt here." They came apart for a bit, then back together. "Leave the room at your own risk."

She looked at him. He appeared serious, but he'd been pushing Seth at her all year. "What gives?" she asked. "Why are you the one passing this on? Why not Alex or Bridget?" She spun away from him and then back.

He caught her hand and pulled her in. He was stronger than he looked. "Alex and Bridget think I owe you something of an apology." Releasing her, he continued dancing. "So I was picked to pass you the message. You may have noticed we're never all out here at the same time." He was right. At least two of them were always sitting out dances... and had been at dances all year. And while Alex and Keisha and Malcolm played sports, the others didn't; they were in the stands, watching. Football. Volleyball. Swimming. Otherwise they were the nerds and geeks. She'd barely noticed until Teddy said that, but there was at least one of the nine near her at all events. "The enemy would prefer to arrange it happening at a public event such as this one. Ego, we think."

"Great. So what am I supposed to do? NOT come to events?"

"It'd be easiest if you simply acknowledged the truth, admitted you're in love with Death, and started coming to these things with Seth," he replied with a grin. "Then he'd be the one primarily looking out for your safety and the rest of us could relax. And given his power, no one and nothing in its right mind would come after you as long as you were with him."

"You are just an ass, Theodore Pope. Get the fuck away from me. And stay out of my head! You and your little brain-dead minions!" She stormed off the dance floor and over to her table. She downed what was left of her latest sprite, grabbed her purse—and why, she wondered, doesn't female formalwear include decent pockets?—and without a backward glance left the auditorium.

"Angela! Wait!" she heard Bridget shout.

She paused briefly in the darkened corridor, then started walking. One of the other doors to the auditorium opened and Marcus came out. She barely glanced at him as she pulled out her phone to call her parents and get picked up. Her gait was getting awkward in these stupid heels, and who came up with the torture devices anyway?

"Angela? Are you okay? What's wrong?" she heard Marcus calling to her from behind but didn't answer him.

"Mom? Can you come get me? I just got in a fight with someone," she said as she heard Marcus approaching softly.

"Of course, honey, I'll be right there. We can have some tea and discuss what happened," she replied.

She clicked off the phone. "Marcus I'm sorry. I really don't feel like being social tonight. Please, go back have fun."

He stopped and looked at her with an odd expression on his face. "Ok. Mind if I punch Teddy's lights out for being a jerk? What'd he do, try to take up where his little buddy Seth left off?"

"No, nothing like that. He just pissed me off."

"Do you want me to wait with you? I can do that," he said.

"No, thanks. I'll be fine. I just don't feel like being in there and social and dancing anymore. I'm sorry."

"Okay, your call." He strode away. When she heard the door close as she stared off into the night, another voice came.

"Thought he'd never go back in." Bridget phased into visibility, almost like some sort of transporter beam and not someone dropping an invisibility spell. She looked at Angela's expression. "Stealth enchantment. Covers all five senses. One of Seth's developments, actually.

"Angela, I'm sorry about Teddy. He's grumping it up back there, so I don't know what happened. Doesn't really matter, but was he able to pass on Seth's warning to you?"

"Yeah, he did." She looked around. No one else was out here, naturally. "You can go back in to, you know. I already called Mom, she'll be here soon enough."

"That isn't going to happen until you're in that car going home, but I can go back into stealth. We don't have to talk if you'd rather not, of course. But I'm not leaving a friend alone when some madman wants to kill her. The others can protect the dance, and as far as Pat's concerned, I'm in the bathroom." She gave her a crooked smile.

"Do you want to tell me who, yet?" she asked, still steaming. If Bridget still wouldn't tell her…

"Elmer Mather," was the calm, quick reply.

"That doesn't help."

"Sorry. You know the phrase "speak of the devil and he appears"? We're pretty sure he's attuned himself to the name he's currently using. I don't think he's going make an appearance if we speak it—not with me standing here, the other seven less than two hundred feet away, and Seth watching his scrying TV for problems—but he might. He'd certainly start paying attention, and his scrying ability is at least as good as ours if not better. He'd be able to direct his minion better."

"Scrying TV?"

"He's put some focus devices scattered around the school, and the eight of us are wearing others. He can use the remote to switch between them. He didn't see any real benefit in using a crystal ball or a mirror, the way Jennifer initially did. So he enchanted a television."

"So how many of those focus devices are in the girls' showers?" She asked. "He is a boy."

Bridget grinned. "He is, and yes he likes girls. But to the best of my knowledge, none. We've done a search for them just about every day. We've found a few of Teddy's, a few more of Solly's and one of Alex's, and we remove them. We've never found one of Malcolm's or Seth's, though. It could always be that they're simply being better at stealth than we think they are, but I don't think so. Malcolm spends a lot of time around people not wearing much anyway. Seth… you're not going to believe this, but he usually respects privacy. If he put one in there it would be because he thought it was needed.

"And it's not like we haven't put some in their showers." She admitted with a blush.

"You have?" Angela asked, blushing a bit herself at the thought. "Anything good?" she asked smiling even as her cheeks practically glowed.

"Depends on your point of view. They're almost as good at finding ours as we are at finding theirs, you know. The difference is the personalities.

Seth doesn't care. He'll leave them up and wave at us as he kills them. Malcolm doesn't really care, either, but if we want them back we need to get them from the bottom of the tanks in the bio lab. I've seen Alex and Solly put on shows before they remove them, and the illusions Teddy has them show us tend to be televangelists' sermons.

"But from the ones who don't suspect a thing? Yeah, you might say so. You might just say so. " And she grinned again. "It's a game between us and the guys, and we're winning. We think. If Seth and Malcolm are participating, we don't know about it. In which case, they're winning."

"Any chance I could, ah, watch with you some time?" She asked.

"I suppose that might be doable. Fair warning, though—we can never guarantee when one will be found, so we don't really have a way to be sure how much we'll see."

"No, you don't," came a male voice, Seth's voice. Angela looked around wildly. Bridget's green eyes glowed as she looked around, and she'd wriggled her ring-clad fingers as if to stretch the muscles in them.

"Don't bother. You're right next to one of my foci, and double clicking the mute button lets me project through it. But a very interesting conversation, Bridget."

"Ok, Seth, what'll it take to buy your silence?" Bridget said in a very get down to business tone.

"Macaria is lonely. Can you help find a mate for her?"

A slow smile spread across Bridget's face, and she nodded. "Oh, absolutely, Seth. I'll be happy to help."

"Who's Macaria?"

"In Greek mythology, the goddess of a blessed death. Or a daughter of Heracles. To Seth, the condor he saved. She's been devoted to him ever since."

"You mean… the condor we saw over Monterey Bay?"

"Was the same bird as was flying over all the games, yes." Bridget confirmed. She shrugged. "You should see him when he's trying to make an impression. Pale horse, black robe, scythe in hand, trailing smoke, black bloodhounds running beside him… pretty awesome."

"Thanks, Bridget," Seth's voice said. "Main reason I actually decided to speak up was that I haven't noticed any assassins even with the overlays

I've applied. They may not be there yet. Or he may have simply disguised them well. I'll remain vigilant. And let you get back to your conversation."

"Um, Seth? DO you have any foci we've missed in the showers?"

"Did you know about this one?"

"No, but we don't sweep the rest of the school as often as we sweep the showers."

"Hmm" was his only reply.

"Damn. I think we're going to need to do something."

"So he does have some?"

"We still don't know. He didn't say," Bridget pointed out to her. "Seth's fairly good at lying by omission and getting people to draw the wrong conclusions from their own prejudices." She paused. "His mom's an attorney."

"Enough about him," Angela said firmly. "When do you want to get together for Bio again?"

Bridget pulled out her own phone. "Owners meeting after school for the Martian and Venusian projects on Monday. Geometry and English Tuesday… How about Wednesday? Wednesday looks good."

"Martian and Venusian projects? What are those?" Angela asked. They'd mentioned something about it at Homecoming but she'd never got around to asking. Just as well, she supposed. They probably wouldn't have told her.

"Do you know what terraforming is?" Bridget asked.

"Um, not really. I've heard the term in some old Star Trek episodes, but that's about it. Dad likes Sulu."

"Ok. Basically terraforming is taking a planet and making liveable, like Earth—or, in Latin, Terra. With me so far?"

"Yes… wait, you're planning to do that to Mars and Venus?"

"Got it in one. We can't do it yet. One of the reasons we keep testing ourselves is to improve our abilities, grow what we can do. We're not sure if we'll need amplifiers or not. We're pretty sure we'll need to do it by stages, and one of those is to speed up Venus. Atmospheric transformations, temperature adjustments."

"Wow, you guys are really ambitious."

"A large part of it is a desire to transfer people off Earth, to quit taxing the resources here. If we're able to do that, it'll make averting climate change here a lot easier." A distant look came to her before she noticed the hybrid silver car pulling up.

"And here's your mother." She paused and her eyes glittered. "Yes, it is your mom, and the car is safe." At Angela's disbelieving expression, she chuckled. "Seth just suggested that an attack might come in a way like that, so I made sure it wasn't actually happening."

"How paranoid is he, anyway? My mom?"

"Could happen. Remember Salerno's? He knows more about ways to die than the rest of us," Bridget replied, totally seriously. "See you Monday!"

Angela shook her head as she was getting into her mother's car. Why would anyone, even a goth like Seth, spend so much time on death? It was positively creepy, even if it did seem to be useful to her today.

"What went wrong, honey?" her mother asked, concerned, after about fifteen minutes in the car.

Her parents still didn't know about the attacks targeting her. Mentioning them would help. It was fairly simple why, she hadn't told them. It was hard to say why she hadn't told them, but she had to admit that Alex and Bridget were probably right about anyone believing they were doing real honest to god magic. And unlike Bridget, she couldn't do any herself, so she couldn't simply prove it to them. And it wasn't time to tell them yet. She looked out the open sunroof. Damn. She could see a caped figure on a horse *in the sky*. Was Seth escorting her home?

"Do you remember telling you about Teddy? The boy who's been insisting that Seth and I are an unacknowledged couple?"

"Uh-huh. Was That Boy at the dance?" she asked, using her name for Seth.

"No, Mom. Seth wasn't there. He hasn't been at any of the dances, actually. But Teddy was. He came with Carmen. Some of his friends thought he owed me an apology, so he asked me to dance. And I didn't want to be rude, so I said okay. And at first it was fine, but then he went back to normal, saying that I should start dating Seth. And it really got me mad. I didn't hit him or anything. I left the dance floor, got my things, and called you."

"Oh, honey. " Mom said as they proceeded. They lived on the exterior of one of the hill streets, in a little cul-de-sac court. There'd been a lot of discussion, early in the year, if she shouldn't simply bike to school. She'd wanted to be around friends, so she took the bus. And, of course, biking would have been out of the question tonight. She stayed quiet a little while longer as she entered their driveway. As she got out of her mom's car, she looked back. The figure on that impossible horse was still there, just sort of hovering. He realized she'd seen him, raised his scythe in salute, and turned the horse away. She was home.

They went in past the atrium and found Dad still up having tea in the breakfast nook. The teakettle on hot plate and cream and sugar were out. "It's decaf, dear, don't worry. What happened? I thought Marcus seemed like a nice enough boy."

"It wasn't Marcus, dear. It was that Teddy boy."

"Really? Honey, you've been ignoring him all year. What set you off here?"

"I don't know..." Even to her, her voice sounded petulant, like somewhere she knew what had been the problem but couldn't bring herself to admit it. Her parents shared a glance. "Maybe it was because usually when he was going on about it, I thought he was doing it to give Seth a hard time, not me. Seth was always right there, waiting for a class, and telling him to knock it off. In a bored voice, y'know, that made Teddy want to keep going and be even more of a jerk than he normally is, like he was trying to draw a reaction from Seth.

"But I think I'm OK now. Bridget came out and waited with me and distracted me from what was going on inside. God bless girlfriends" she said.

"Are you just tired? Do you think maybe some extra sleep will help? You've been staying up fairly late most nights this week working on your homework, and you did have a swim meet this morning and afternoon," Dad suggested. It wasn't out of the question but she wasn't actually feeling tired.

"Maybe. I think I'm going to go to my room, change, and maybe see about getting some sleep."

"Okay, Honey. Have a good night." Dad said.

She was in her room, listening to music on her phone, when a call came in. It was Carmen. "Hey, girl, what's up? Teddy's being a grouch over you storming off, and with the exception of his little groupies no one seems to think you're to blame. So what happened? Everyone seems to think you screamed something different at him, really."

"Oh, I don't know. He was being Teddy—y'know, suggesting that Creepo and I are secretly in love and a total couple? Something about it just set me off tonight" she replied.

"Um, Ange, I really hate to suggest this… but there's nothing to what he says, is there? I mean, it's totally cool with me if there is, and you certainly can date whoever you want, but…"

Angela laughed. "No, Carmen, really, there is absolutely nothing of the sort going on! I don't like him, he doesn't like me. He's still the perve who put his hand down my bra. He's still dreary Gothy McGoth, y'know? And even he tells Teddy to quit it when he starts in on me."

"Okay, cool. Have a good night! Everyone's worried a bit about you, so I'll tell them you're fine."

"You have a good time, too, Carmen. But don't tell Teddy I'm fine. There's absolutely no reason he has to know that, is there?" Angela asked.

Carmen laughed. "No, no there's not. Let him stew with his groupies."

"If you're going to do that, would you mind hooking up with Marcus for the rest of the dance? I feel a little guilty about leaving him all by himself," she said.

"Marcus? You're letting me have Marcus? Cool beans. He's dreamy. Thanks!" Carmen replied. Angela was a bit surprised at how eagerly Carmen went for Marcus. Had Teddy asked her simply as part of the plan to protect her? She'd ask Bridget about it on Monday.

She fielded several more calls from her friends checking up on her. None from the nine, but she hadn't really expected any after Bridget had waited with her and Seth had actually escorted her home. On a flying horse, no less, but it was a nice gesture. Creepy as well as nice. The music played. The birds were angry. She didn't really get to sleep at any more parentally determined "reasonable' hour than she had the rest of the week, but tomorrow was Sunday and Dad wasn't really anymore inclined to go to church now than he was during the NFL season. He'd gotten very enthusiastic about the Golden State Football League, especially when he'd found out that the Unicorns were actively recruiting his football playing daughter. And Mom liked Bridget's Stableboys. So when the boringest of the boring was scheduled for the pulpit, she was fairly sure no one was going to be trying to get her to go to church in the morning, and she drifted into dreamland.

Angela woke to the sounds of sobbing. She was with about twelve other kids, and she was the oldest by at least four years. Leather cords bound her hands, and as she looked she saw cords on most of the other kids. Three had plastic ties instead, and one girl even had handcuffs. The floor was concrete... stained, cracked concrete, and the room stank of motor oil and fear and gasoline. A garage, then. She looked around and noticed a shovel left with some rakes. "Can you help me up? I think I can cut these on that shovel, and see about getting you guys free too. I'm Angela. Who are you?"

"I'm George." "Mikey" "Erminee" "Kitty" "Jenny" "Sarah". "I'm Angela, too!" "Jorge" "Jerry" "Mackenzie" "Kaylee" "Mulan".

"OK, let's see about getting out of here," she said, rubbing the leather cords on the shovel blade. It was dull, of course. But one of the cords snapped, and that was all she really needed to get them off. Her helper was the little blond girl who called her self. "Erminee". "Hermione?" she asked. Only made sense she'd be named for a Harry Potter character.

"Yeth," she said. "Erminee Goddard." She looked about five.

"Thank you, Hermione." Now that she was free, she needed to figure out where they were. "Has anyone been in to feed you? Give you water? Anything like that?"

"No" they chorused. Right. They can't have been here long, or the kids would be clamoring that they were hungry or thirsty. She started undoing those bonds that she could. Well, she'd get the rest of them when she could.

"Anyone know where we are?"

"We're up in the hills, I think," said the other Angela. "I peeked through that window over there, and all the roads are dirt. The buildings are kind of old and just about all thick wood."

"Yeah, that's where we are. I think we may be up at the White Hill Christian Academy; my brother's on your team," said Jerry, "and I came up to watch the game." She looked at him again and recognized Atlee Olafssen's little brother. The blond boy was, like the other Angela, around ten.

"Okay, thanks, Jerry, Angela. We need to get out of here. You guys think you can walk down the hill? Hike to freedom?"

"What do they want with us?"

"I don't know. But since they're not supposed to have us, we should take ourselves back and go down the hill."

"Why don't we take a twuck? You can dwive us!" Hermione said.

Angela blinked. Yes, she was fifteen now. She'd had a few lessons. They could try it. "Do you know where the keys are? Because hotwiring a truck is something I don't know how to do."

"No..."

"Well maybe they've been stupid and left keys in here. Look all around." This was a long shot at best. She'd probably need help; she *physically* couldn't call the cops. She closed her eyes and tried reaching out to the people who might be able to turn up regardless.

"Oh, Alex, any chance of you showing up? Please? Bridget? Can you hear me? Dawn? I know we don't talk much, but can you help me? Malcolm? Keisha? Jennifer? Solomon?" She needed help. That was obvious. She needed to try harder. Even "Teddy? Can you hear me?" A crash of doors and the startled screams of the kids let her know that someone else was there. She looked up and saw several large boys she recognized from the White Hill football team.

"The Reverend wants to see you now, whore."

The big boys from the football team dragged her into the church. Several other boys retied the kids.

She struggled but her mind was flailing around in terror as the Reverend's mouth opened and she saw the fangs. She started praying and the Reverend laughed. "I am the servant of God here. He has given you unto me." He came forward.

She continued struggling, but the Reverend grabbed her right arm and used his strength…and god he was strong, stronger than the boys of the football team, stronger than anyone she'd ever encountered despite his spindly old limbs… to bind her left arm to his body while his other hand pulled her hair and neck to the side. She tried to head butt him but his grip was far too strong. She could feel his fangs on her neck, the teeth of his lower jaw scraping her skin right before he plunged in his fangs. She whimpered as he began to drink her blood.

A memory flashed into her mind. Alex's words. She whispered them desperately; Alex hadn't heard her, nor Bridget or Dawn. Maybe she just had to say the spell properly. "Seth, I am in the church of the White Hill Christian Academy. Seth, I entreat your aid."

A pale glowing figure coalesced in front of her "Not my granddaughter you monster! Stay away from her or feel my wrath!" The reverend released her and stumbled back away from the ghostly presence. "More help is on the way sweetie. I could just get here quickest."

A single figure moved in the dark outside when the light suddenly erupted and the Reverend slowly turned, saying, "Welcome, Mr. Menendez. Your exploits on the field will be the stuff of quashed legend…"

"Sorry to disappoint," drawled a voice from the swirling blackness, even in the brightest light, and the two men at the doors of the church dropped like sacks of potatoes. "The General's still gathering his forces. You produce plenty for me." She knew that voice. Alex hadn't come for her, despite the fact she knew she'd somehow gotten through. Or… had she gotten through to Alex at all?

The drawling figure looked at the White Hill players. "Boys, run while you can. He's never going to make you like him. He can't." The figure cocked his head. "He doesn't know how. He doesn't even know how he screwed up and made himself like this."

The Reverend looked at the figure in swirling blackness. "Who in God's name are you? There's only one practitioner of the arts in this county! And that is Alex Menendez!"

"Release Angela and the others. And leave. This is ours. You are not welcome here. And I will not destroy you. Your choice." The big football players of White Hill Christian sneered at him and advanced on him, cracking their knuckles and ready to pound him flat. A light flashed at the heart of the darkness.

Another ghost manifested, obviously a small girl. "Why Reverend? Why did you kill me? Peter, why do you help him? Why are you helping him hurt and kill more people?" and players stopped in their tracks, one of them breaking out in what was obviously a cold sweat, trembling, and saying the name "Josie" over and over again.. Boards ripped from the walls and floor to wrap themselves around the Reverend's minions. The two men at the door rose. Their expressions were blank, and the windows smashed as more figures spilled into the church, and still more came in through the holes ripped open by the absent boards. Shards of glass tore at their clothes and their flesh, but they paid no attention to the torn clothing and their flesh did not bleed. Zombies had risen and came after the boys the Reverend was relying on.

In the battle that followed, Angela had only thought she'd understood what one of the nine could do when Alex faced Frankenstein's Turkey. Spirits manifested—young, old. All of them accused the Reverend of killing them. She recognized Sarah Campbell and a girl from the movie theater, and the man who murdered the cheerleaders. However the Reverend had commanded them in life, here in Death they were his enemies. Their condemnations and accusations swirled around the room in a terrifying cacophony, and the Reverend's face blanched. Worse was their effect on his minions, for many of them fled in terror. Horror suffused her at the crackling black beams her savior was tossing around in a way that sheared clean through thick wooden beams, and the clear dark shields that shrugged aside the Reverend's white beams. Adults—teachers and coaches, and faculty—that were devoted to the Reverend came to help. The black cloaked figure glanced at them and they fell…only to rise again moments later under his control. Fire and lightning blasted the room. The Reverend tried to control the zombies and send them to attack her rescuer, but that wasn't working at all, and they pounded at his defenses to the point of their own destruction. Boards ripped from the walls to dance across the path of the Reverend's beams and shield her from some of his strikes. Zombies held struggling football players, hauling them out of the church, and ignored her, until the figure extended his own shields around her. Pews ripped out of the floor to wrap around boys and men and absorb the Reverend's attacks. As some of Angela's terror and horror leached away, she noticed the two of them appeared to be fairly well balanced. With the zombies moving the football players out of the church, she made a move out of those protective shields.

She'd found a football one of the players had brought in, rolled over to it, picked it up and threw. She wasn't as accurate as someone like Alex who practiced every day, but they'd run plays where she was supposed to throw it. In the movies, the bad guy always forgot to protect himself against physical distractions. She looked expectantly as the ball bounced off the Reverend's shields a foot away from him. "Did you truly think I was that foolish, girl?" His next release of energy crumbled the floor where she'd been standing and turned the pews to dust; she found herself floating down as the black cloaked figure's blast hit was deflected towards the ceiling. She ducked behind him and considered. She didn't want to touch the Reverend's energy barrier; she had no idea what that would do. But the bouncing football gave her an idea. The Reverend had returned his attention to his opponent as cracks appeared in his own defenses.

Angela climbed the rafters of the old church. It was built years ago, but the deflected blasts had opened up holes, and the ceiling tiles had come through. The tiles were clay and slate; she started grabbing tiles and flinging them down directly on the Reverend. The tiles, like the rocks, didn't inflict much damage, but her rescuer's blast was timed to take advantage of it. Seth had said that the shields could only take so much damage, so she might as well let gravity increase it. Wider cracks appeared, and then a second blast shattered them.

"Well, vampire. Time to die. Permanently." Her rescuer didn't even blast him this time. The Reverend was flung against the giant cross on the wall and stuck there. He didn't scream; the vampire seemed entirely unaffected by the fact that it was a cross. Then he was ripped apart in a gory explosion of energies. The zombies holding the football players collapsed, their job done.

"Reverend Johnson is no more. Neither are any of his minions. Find your own way. If you bother us again, I will treat you as I did his minions.

Are there any questions?" the black robed figure addressed the boys of White Hill Christian. Many of them were shaking their heads and looking at the figure in pure terror. Whatever they'd expected, a zombie apocalypse was not it. Neither was a spirit assault out of "Raiders of the Lost Ark". The figure raised his hand and the boys vanished, back to their homes and parents to figure out their next move in life.

Angela couldn't figure out how she knew that.

After that, she wondered how many of them would retain their faith in anything religious, after serving a vampire… who was the most important religious figure in their lives.

The swirling black-cloaked figure moved slowly as he turned to face her. His stiffness, his pain, his weariness were evident as he stood, the crackling energies no longer providing that weird black light, but it looked like he'd been in the line all game. She saw dust coming up the hill, even here in the night. The pieces of Reverend Johnson weren't even dripping from where the last blast of energies had ripped him apart. He stood there for maybe a minute, maybe less. Angela still couldn't see his face, but somehow, she knew Seth had come to save her.

Seth looked at her. His voice spoke in her head. *<Thank you for distracting him, Angela. Alex and some of the football team will be here shortly; that's their dust. The police will be here in about an hour. The others can't recognize me, do not see me, and have no idea what happened. Johnson's people are gone; you'll be safe until the cops arrive to take you home. I was never here. If something does happen that you need help with, bespeak Toranos or Chiomara, and he or she will come.>* He vanished. But the other kids were coming out now. She could think on it all later. Even though… she understood that when Seth had said "gone" he meant dead. She'd watched him kill the White Hill teachers with little more than a glance. Dawn's warning to Alex about what Seth could have done to the team… A conversation with him, months ago rushed back to her…

Her grandmother's ghost came over to her. "Not the most polite of young men, but a good child. I need to go, Angie-chan."

"On to heaven? Thank you for staying a little longer."

Her expression saddened. "Oh, not that, Angie-chan. I'm… memories, given form and voice by the will of the wizard, but just for a time. He used you as a conduit for me, but the energy to keep me here is coming from you now. He's having me explain this to you before the time limit he placed on me gives out. So you understand." She dispersed as Angela watched. Then the team was there, piling out of half a dozen cars, looking ready to pound someone. Sometimes she forgot just how big the offensive line was. Alex got out of a back seat. He looked almost as sweaty and tired as he would after a game. He started issuing orders—she could see why Seth had called him the General. Everyone did what he was told, fanning out looking for anyone else who might be around. Some of them went over to the kids and started talking to them. Alex loped over to her, his expression serious.

"I think I see why you were so concerned about what Seth was capable of," she remarked quietly as he came up. He nodded.

"I hope so. Death is his domain, and he can kill with a thought, almost, and if he lost control it wouldn't be pretty. And if you remember the stories from Juvenile hall when he was there… that was him. He dealt with gangs coming after him by inflicting the Black Death on them. And polio, leprosy, flu, cholera. Whatever it took. To tell you the truth, Ange, that's what I was really afraid of. He's been practicing by helping Bridget with invasive species. Wild boar. Striped bass. Feral goats. Iceplant. Their activities have made the news several times." He paused and took a deep breath, looking her directly in the eyes as he did so.

"But… that's animals. And plants…" she protested, but she almost expected Alex's next words.

"Angela, you've been getting A's in biology, and I know you've been hanging out with Bridget all year. *It doesn't matter*. WE are animals. It might be different psychologically to kill another human. Physically, it's not. Kill the brain and kill the human, the pig, or the fish.

"Incidentally, Ange, I know Seth already talked to you, but I've been spreading the word that I got a text from you as the reason I knew where you'd been taken. Why don't you go get some coffee and we'll wait for the cops?" Angela nodded and headed off to get something to drink when she shook her head and looked back at Alex. He was already over and talking to little Hermione Goddard, smiling at her and getting her to laugh, some of the other kids were around him as well.

Had Alex given her a low intensity command to be obeyed… and she'd broken through the enchantment? Coffee did sound good, though, after the hours she'd been confined. She shrugged to herself. Now that she noticed it, she saw little hints of purple all over. Alex was remaining in command—even when some of the team who'd come with him were seniors—by resorting to his magic. Even with the battle between Seth and the Reverend, they shouldn't have arrived this quickly, so obviously Alex had cheated. She noticed he was also keeping people from asking awkward questions no one wanted to answer.

She got her paper cup of coffee and went back over to Alex. "Alex," she said sotto voce, "never do that again."

He turned to look at her. "Sorry, Ange. It's easier to not make exceptions in this. I'm coordinating every one and dulling their curiosity at the same time. I'm coordinating, not controlling people, and you already know what happened. Not to mention trying to control YOU would take a lot of effort I can't really afford to spend. Seth doesn't do things half way, does he?"

From outside, the old church was in even worse shape. The spire hung upside down, barely attached by warped boards. Holes gaped in the ceiling and the walls. Many of them were the precise diameter of the beams they'd been using to fight, but others were jagged, broken when a beam had undermined something. The zombies had smashed through the windows, torn doors off hinges, and even burst through a couple of spots in the walls where Seth or the Reverend had blasted holes, as well as the places from which Seth had ripped boards to wrap around the Reverend's allies.

Whatever. White Hill Christian Academy was as dead as the Reverend, maybe more so. The teachers and faculty and coaches had died under Seth's pitiless gaze. A few bodies remained of their zombies, but Seth had hurled them at the Reverend's defenses, using them up to weaken them just a little bit more. Had the Reverend even obtained the property legally? Was there anyone at all left who might keep the horrid place running?

Alex continued, "We need to keep people out of there. It could collapse at any time, at any moment. It looks like other Academy kids are getting restless; I need to deal with them and keep the peace as best I can. Can you make sure none of the little kids try to go back in? Please?"

She nodded. Keeping the kids out was important. She could do that. It wasn't a command; it was a request.

CHAPTER

12

After she got home, she lay awake a long time. The cops had taken a statement from her and let her go home. She'd heard them talking about putting out an all points bulletin for Reverent Johnson, but that would obviously be pointless. She'd watched Seth rip him apart. What Bridget and Malcolm had shown her in Monterey… what Alex had shown her on the hike… none of it came close to what she'd seen of Seth that night. He hadn't been concealing his power, not tonight. It had been open, in your face, not caring who saw, and she couldn't shake the idea that despite her dropping the planks on the Reverend, Seth would have won faster if he hadn't been protecting her. His open power was terrifying. And somehow darkly glorious. No Hollywood wizard could match what she'd been at the heart of as he ripped the Reverend to pieces.

The cops had said that the Reverend's journal said something about girls playing sports being an abomination against the Lord, that she and Dani and some of the other girls scattered around the county playing on boys teams were whores to be destroyed, but also that he had fixated on her when he hadn't killed her on the bus crash. He couldn't understand how she kept surviving his repeated attempts to kill her.

Angela knew. Alex had told her in an ambulance on Lucas Valley Road. Malcolm had repeated it on the back of a killer whale in Monterey Bay. Seth. Seth, Goth of the Dead. He had identified the danger to her all the way back in August. He'd passed the warning on to her through Alex. He'd warned his eight friends, and they'd been keeping an eye on her all year. Bridget, Malcolm, Alex, Teddy, Jennifer, Dawn, Solomon, Keisha, and Seth himself had rescued her at various times. She'd saved herself a couple of times, but hadn't even realized that's what she was doing at the time.

The alarm went off, it was time for school. She rolled over and got to her feet, before Mom could come and get her up for school. It was time to face the day. Face school.

Bridget plopped down next to her on the school bus. She surprised Angela; Bridget didn't normally take this bus, and Angela had been staring pensively out the window. "Hi Angela."

"What are you doing on this bus?" Angela asked, startled. She wasn't sure she wanted to be talking to anyone.

"I stayed with Jenny last night," nodding at Jenny O'Neil, who'd secured her own place next to Malcolm. Jenny was a slightly built redhead who favored long dresses, an uber nerd who tutored sophomores and juniors, while Malcolm's brown hair was streaked with green highlights from being on the swim team. Right, she thought. Mr. Merboy. He hadn't lost a race all year and wasn't likely to, given what she'd seen of him in Monterey Bay. At least they normally rode this bus. But they were two of the Nine, of course. Maybe not as overwhelmingly powerful as Seth. Somehow it suddenly got less noisy.

"I hear you had an eventful weekend," Bridget started. "Do you wanna to talk about it?" She looked at her with concern.

"No, not really. Still processing, y'know? I mean… wait, how did you know? I just got the kids out of there and went straight to bed when I got home!"

"Seth called last night. We all met out at Fort Cronkite, down at one of the coves where no one goes."

"So now what? I'm expected to be his date to the year-end dance? Black knight gets the girl?" Angela's indignant rant was just getting started when Bridget snorted and rolled her eyes.

"You really don't know him at all, do you?" She leaned in, green eyes locking with brown. "Angela, Seth will be the first to say you owe him nothing, and I don't think he'll ever ask anyone on a date. He'd probably decline an invitation! And no, you don't owe him a date. But you might want to think a bit more deeply, Angela. Seth didn't have to respond to your calling on him. He could have stayed home rather than rescue someone who's been treating him like crap all year long." She paused and pulled up her bag. "You lived through a zombie apocalypse this weekend. If you're not clued in enough now to talk to him, you never will be. Most mornings you can find him…"

"In the library, I know." She paused. She didn't spend hours on end figuring out where Seth was. "Wait, how do I know that? I mean, he lives there, yeah, but…"

"You'll have to ask Seth. Malcolm and I suggested you talk to him in Santa Cruz. Alex suggested it after the team hike. It's time you talked to him and understood." She looked past Angela. "Oh, look, school." Bridget got up and made her way off the bus. It had seemed like a shorter ride than normal… she glanced at her phone. It had been. They should still be on the road… for another twenty minutes. Jenny and Malcolm were drinking cranberry juice boxes as they made their way off.

Angela walked down the corridors full of students at lockers, talking to their friends, flirting, kissing their significant others. Rather than stop at her own locker, she headed straight for the library. A corridor down from it she spotted Mike Smith and Kevin Pastorini. They looked to be up to something. "Hey Ange! " they motioned her over. They showed her a bloated balloon filled with liquid. "The pervert's hiding in there. When he comes out we're going to hit him with this. Guess what's in it?"

"Pig piss!" They burst out laughing. Her hands went to her hips.

"Get out of here. I'm going in to make peace with him. He's already told Alex he's not putting up with any more from the team. He's been watching out for me all year and I've been treating him like crap. That ends today." She strode past them and kept going. An awful stench came from behind her. Looking back she saw the balloon had burst on them… and she saw Alex disappearing around a corner.

The doors to the library were open. Angela had never used them much—usually only if she were meeting Bridget for a study session or something—but this time she was looking for someone else. She took the stairs up to the second floor, where the darkest, mustiest stacks were. She looked down each stack before she came to the one with her quarry, where the light was so dim she could barely see the titles on the shelves much less something on a page. A small two-person desk was at the other end. She bit her lip. Planning to come in here and confront him was one thing. Now she was here. She was actually going to do it, and her stomach was in knots. She briefly thought of asking Bridget or Alex, see if they'd tell her that she was right, or that she was way off base, but…

He looked up at her. He arched an eyebrow. "I can't very well stay away from you when you come hunting me down." He didn't seem surprised to see her, more like he'd been expecting her. He probably was. The nine had demonstrated they had ways of communicating.

She looked at him, really looked at him for the first time, in ever. His face was pale, the pale of a boy who preferred to sit inside and read than do anything outside, and his hair dark brown. His lips were thin, his belly large. He'd started to grow and fill out over the school year; his belly wasn't quite as large anymore. He was wearing a black shirt, a dress shirt, with pearlescent buttons and long sleeves, comfortable Dockers, again black, and black tennis shoes. A crystal ended, mini black flashlight hung from a silvered chain around his neck. So did a little silver disc from a renaissance faire. The crystal glowed in the dim light of the library, but the switch on the flashlight was in the off position. It lit the silver disc enough to see the wreathed skull stamped into it.

She took a deep breath, and spoke quietly. "You once told me 'death is my domain'. This weekend I lived through a zombie movie, complete with people I saw die get back up and join the zombies, except that they all fell over dead when we were safe. I was abducted and fed on by a vampire, and you ripped him to pieces. My grandmother's ghost told me that you were the one that summoned her to my defense. I called your name from miles away and you came for me. Alex and Bridget both insist that when you put your hand down my bra that you weren't copping a feel, but I'd never believe what you were actually doing." He kept looking at her, barely blinking. She went on, "When you told the cops and Ms. Lee that you were checking for a heart beat, you were lying." Seth cocked his head.

Angela closed her eyes. "You weren't seeing if I was alive. You'd checked my neck pulse; you already knew I wasn't. You were raising me from the dead." She felt something come together behind her back, stretching forward to where Seth sat. She opened her eyes to see him put his bottle of root beer down.

"Yes, I did." He was completely calm about it, and a little sigh seemed to escape him. "At the risk of wounding your ego, the concentration I needed to bring you back, even with skin to skin contact at heart and brain, was more than enough to occupy all my attention. I didn't even notice." He kept up his calm regard of her as he spoke, and volunteered nothing more. This was her meeting.

"Did you have to touch me there?"

"Strictly speaking, no. I didn't have to touch you at all. I'd already tired myself going incorporeal to keep from getting hurt when the bus crashed and switching back, and that's the easiest way to restore life."

"What did you just do?" Might as well keep it away from slightly less strange territory.

"I enclosed us in a private bubble. No one can hear us talking. If it makes you feel better, it's not stopping you from walking away." He continued to speak calmly.

She giggled nervously. "Not really." He shrugged. "You could probably stop me from walking away if you really wanted to." He appraised her for a moment,

"If I wanted to." Despite the privacy bubble, he spoke quietly and with complete confidence.

She spent several long moments looking at him. He sipped his root beer and continued to look back calmly at her. "Are you a god?" she blurted out.

A smile crossed his face, the first real expression she'd seen since she walked in here, and an eyebrow popped up and down as he said simply, "Yes."

Her eyes widened in shock and she fell to her knees. "Jesus Christ!"

He started laughing. "Jocks. Wouldn't get a movie reference to save their silly lives." He leaned forward. "No, Angela. We're not gods. Why do you ask that"?

"You seem so much more powerful than Alex or Bridget."

"Ah. I'm not, really. Jennifer is the most powerful of us. What I am, given the nature of what I'm particularly good at, is the *deadliest* of us. That's why we were kept as reserves at Halloween. Alex is good at enhancing things, and people, at getting people to do what he wants them to. He doesn't really like doing that so he relies more on his personal charisma. It makes him one hell of an effective leader. Bridget is good with life and living things. If the Reverend had been facing her all his minions would have been writhing on the floor, their muscles locked up. I needed to bring zombies to keep them distracted if I didn't want to kill them.

"Getting back to your original question, as far as we can tell, there aren't any gods. We traveled the world last summer, and we LOOKED. The legends and myths of gods appear to be tales of practitioners in history, at best. We're pretty sure that there are more practitioners out there, left overs from history. That's what came at us at Halloween, a nineteenth century practitioner and the monsters she'd made for herself," he said as an aside. "And just stories a lot of the time."

"Even Teddy? He doesn't believe either?"

He snorted and gave her a crooked smile. "Teddy *started* questioning before the rest of us even thought to. Most of us were simply raised without religion in our lives. He thinks the god of the bible is a monster that makes Cthulhu look cuddly. That piety is an act to keep his parents contented, and he still needs to manipulate their minds to keep himself safe. He's convinced they'd kill him if they knew what he was actually capable of doing. There are reasons he's the best of us at illusions."

"God is no more real than unicorns?"

"No, gods are less real than unicorns. What makes you think unicorns aren't real?" He cocked his head at her.

"Oh, come on, Seth. Unicorns?"

"Bridget's made five of them. Her preferred mount, actually. I'm surprised she hasn't shown them to you. I think she's planning for herds, maybe replace mustangs. Solomon's on that project with her."

She remembered the stallions she and Bridget had ridden in Arcata. If those were actually unicorns, not horses, their defensive behavior made a lot more sense. Far more intelligent than horses, understanding the need to work together against what were, obviously in retrospect, unnatural dogs… Wonderingly, she looked up and asked, "What.., how…?

He settled back, understanding her even without the words. "Two years ago last June—so just about three years ago, now—we did something. At first we thought we needed to be together. Then we figured out we could do things on our own. We're not really sure what we're actually doing," he said, back in that calm voice. "We get the effect we want… usually."

"Could Alex have… brought me back?" she asked hesitantly. "Did it have to be you?"

"Death isn't Alex's specialty, the way it is mine, but any of us can do something… usually." He paused to drink his root beer. "There, on the bus? Alex was in no shape to help any one else. He had a stick through his liver, three or four broken bones, cuts all over and gashes from the glass across his chest and forehead, and pieces of the window in his arm. If he weren't as good at healing as he is he'd probably have died. He spent most of his power just getting himself back together. I don't think he could have had the energy to bring someone back that day, not even with skin-to-skin contact at the head and heart. Not even someone who was almost completely uninjured otherwise, as you were."

Angela listened in horror to Seth's recital of Alex's injuries. When she'd come back to herself in the bus, Alex was bloody but not that bad. He certainly didn't have a stick in his guts or any broken bones! Her shock was clearly evident to him. He shook his head.

"Alex has been hurting himself for years, Angela. Sports injuries. Falling out of trees. He's the one who decided to pick up the alligator lizard and got bit. He takes the risks. He's the one to lead us INTO taking the risks. He's better at healing himself than any of the rest of us. You may have noticed his football injuries are never as bad as they seem? By the time you were back, he'd already handled the worst of it. Enough so that he wouldn't even miss any playing time."

"Oh", she said, feeling a little foolish. Seth was right about Alex's getting hurt on the field. Whatever happened he always seemed to be feeling better soon and ready to go back in. And however pain drenched his voice on the bus, he'd been on the field the next week. "Did you two really need 911? Or was all that for my benefit?"

"No. If we'd needed additional help we could have called one of the others, but Alex could have finished healing himself. But it would have been suspicious if we'd walked away from the crash or gotten ourselves out of there. So we stayed and let the ambulances and the cops do their jobs. We don't exactly need the bus, either; you saw me teleport. We're not yet ready to reveal ourselves to the world. If you hadn't kept at it, you wouldn't know, either." His lips twitched. "Of course there were also arguments that we should have simply left you dead."

She shuddered at the reminder. "Seth, can I ask a question?"

"You just did," he replied with a straight face.

She glared at him before she could remember what he'd admitted he was capable of and stop herself. THAT response was just so… so… Seth. "Why did you come? I mean, why not Alex? Or… or…"

"Bridget? Dawn?" He finished for her. "That's simple enough. I heard you. They didn't."

"I don't get it. I mean, I tried to speak to all of the others before I tried you, thinking…"

"Close your eyes and point to me." She rolled her eyes, closed them, and started to point… then shifted to her left arm and pointed the other way. "Open your eyes." Seth was standing several feet down the stacks, and then in a swirl of black was seated back at the desk. "When I brought you back from the dead, it created a bond between us. When you spoke my name, even my ordinary name, in supplication, I heard you. I heard your plea for help. The secret names exist so we can bespeak each other without doing it accidentally. I knew where you were. Just like you knew where I was, here and now. I came to help and left when you were no longer in apparent danger. I think that if we keep interacting, the bond will stay, even strengthen. I've brought a few animals back, and the ones that didn't stick around eventually lapsed."

"You know where I am? What I'm doing? That doesn't make me feel any better about it, Seth. I'm glad it was there and it worked, this weekend, but…"

He leaned back and sipped his root beer again. "No. Doesn't actually work like that. I'm not Santa Claus. I don't see you when you're sleeping or know if you've been bad, or anything else, normally. It requires effort, from either end. You speaking my name trying to get my attention gets me sight and sound of you and what you're hearing and seeing, for a few seconds or as you're holding the line. I can get more and more solid information, if I concentrate on you at the time. I can concentrate myself on you through it and get a bit, but if you're not holding your end it ultimately gives me a headache." He paused and shrugged. "I've been trying to let it lapse all year. All I've been doing with it is knowing how to keep away from you most of the time. If you were wondering if I was spying on you in the shower, the answer's no." She blushed, but that had been a question in her mind. "I'm not sure what happens now that you've called to me and I've responded. None of the animals ever did that. But my guess is that it's enormously strengthened."

Angela considered that but a more pressing question came out. "Is this bond you call it the reason Alex won't ask me out? He thinks that you have some claim on me?" Angela was a little appalled at herself for asking Seth such a personal question, but it just came out. Bridget had at least implied that there was something between Seth and Alex regarding her.

"That. And the fact that he's had a thing for Danielle since six year olds soccer and Pee-Wee football, which has more to do with it, I think. They're finally on the same team." He smiled at her expression and shrugged. "It's not like Alex and I have discussed it. I don't think I have a claim on you, if that's what you're asking. I'm not prince charming and this is an urban fantasy, not a Disney movie. It would be nice if people stopped regarding me as a pervert, but it's probably far enough gone that I'm not going to escape it now."

"Then why was I told to go to you if I wanted answers?"

"Beyond needing to clear the air about what happened on the bus, you mean? The bond that created... It's not a "claim" on you, so much as a *connection*. What it means, going forward, you and I have to decide. And it's a decision better made when we're both clear on what has happened between us."

Angela digested that for a moment. "Seth, was Reverend Johnson really a vampire? You recognized him, and when you did you whipped his ass."

"I destroyed him, Angela. That wasn't a game. My power against his, with survival the only prize," Seth replied seriously. "To answer your question, yes, he was a vampire. I think vampires are mistakes, someone trying to make an immortal and what arises needs to be sustained by blood. As a vampire, his body was dead, sustained by his power. That left it mine to do with as I chose, and once I realized what he was, the fight was a lot easier."

"Seth, can you answer why me? Why did the Reverend devote such time and effort and repeated attempts to destroy ME? I mean, however good I am, I'm just one person on a team. Why keep coming after me? I remember from early in the year some girls dying mysteriously."

"Because he failed, and he didn't understand why, and he got obsessed. Remember how he was expecting Alex? Alex foiled an early attempt on Dani loudly, in a way that no one who can use this power could possibly mistake for something else—he basically took over the agents' minds and sent them back programmed to do a Laurel and Hardy routine. Going after Dani would mean going through Alex. But while Alex was around the first few attempts on you, he wasn't always, and some of the defenses were a lot more subtle. He couldn't figure out how you survived the bus crash, or the hounds in Arcata, or either attack in Santa Cruz. He only knew the hounds and his agents in Santa Cruz died. I'm surprised he didn't realize when I used my power directly"

"I'm not understanding," she admitted.

"In Arcata and Monterey, Bridget's power was used indirectly, on her created or controlled minions. In the theater, Dawn and Solly were concentrating their power on countering what he was doing, but didn't go after the minion he had in the audience. Mine, on the bus and in Santa Cruz, was used on you personally and on the Reverend's minion. If he'd been paying attention, he might have realized that there was another, and that that person had a power potentially even more dangerous to him than what Alex could do." He shrugged. "But he didn't. He thought Alex was his only opposition."

"You keep calling it "power" or "energy". Isn't what you've stumbled across "magic"? I mean…" Her hands spread. What else could it be?

His mouth quirked. "Felarie and I prefer to be a bit more precise. Like I said, we don't really know what we've come across. If it's some sort of magic, I think that we could teach it to others, but as far as I know we can't do that. Or maybe it's something in the people we've tried to teach, or that we're simply not very good teachers. And we've got some internal divisions on if we should teach anyone, and who we should teach if we do. We're being cautious about it."

"Alex said to be cautious about your secret names."

"He was right. It's something of our little secret, and neither Dawn nor I am happy that you know ours. Incidentally, Angoral is still saying we should wipe your mind."

"Please, no! I don't want to lose my memories!" Angela was horrified at the thought.

"Didn't think you would. It's not something anyone really wants to happen to them. I don't think you have anything to worry about. But for your own sake, follow Alex's advice," he replied. "Angoral doesn't seem like he's going to act on his own. Not with a friend of Bridget and Alex. And your bond to me provides its own measure of protection, not only does it strengthen your own mind but I'll know if someone tries tampering with your mind. But if it makes it into school gossip, the votes can change."

"OK. Thanks for the warning. I won't talk about it with anyone but you, Alex, and Bridget." She paused. "A few weeks ago Bridget said someone had been tampering with my mind and someone put a stop to it, and it wasn't her. In fact, she said you stopped it."

"True." He paused. "I noted, through the bond, and stopped it. Someone thought he was being funny."

She'd written 'I'm in love with Death' on her biology worksheet. And the closest thing she'd ever come to a personification of death was sitting in front of her drinking root beer. "What... what... what was he doing? Accessing my deep dark desires that I might not even realize I have? Or something else? And who was it?"

Seth seemed to bite back laughter. "No, he wasn't getting into your deep subconscious. I'm sure that would have triggered a reaction in the bond sooner than it did, and I noticed almost immediately. He was simply messing with your surface thoughts, slipping something in. It wasn't control, it was...suggestion. The Reverend knew how to exert sufficient control over someone to select their actions for them, and send them out to accomplish a mission they wouldn't ordinarily do. To really control someone, we can't be doing anything else, or at least, we can't yet. The turkey was something different. It was a dead thing, and the programming I provided it was established while it was still dead. We can slip in suggestions that make you think something is your idea or get you doing something automatically, triggered to when you let your mind wander, or illusions that get you to react in a certain way. As for who it was…" Alex paused, then shrugged. "Teddy. You may have noticed him doing similar things to you all year? His idea of a joke."

She reflected on her memories, and Seth was right. "Sorry for getting you in trouble. I was wrong about you." She took a deep breath and hitched her backpack up a little higher.

He nodded, as she turned to walk back down the aisle of old books, barely pausing. Then she stopped, and turned, and looked back at him. That hadn't been enough. This was the boy who'd raised her from the dead. Who'd come to save her. Whom she'd cried out to in despair. He wasn't looking at her. He'd already gone back to his book. "Seth?"

He looked up. "Yes?"

She swallowed. "Thank you, Seth. Thank you for my life."

"You're welcome, Angela."

EPILOGUE

<Seth, what's the chemical symbol for gold?> Angela thought loudly.

The voice in her head responded immediately, *<Last June, you found the very idea of the bond between us that lets us even hold this conversation abhorrent. Now you want me to help you cheat on a chemistry quiz?>* Fortunately, the powerful boy wizard—or, as he would say, practitioner—sounded amused in her head rather than angry.

She answered some of the other questions while still talking silently with Seth. *<Well, as long as it's present, I might as well get SOME use out of it,>* she shot back.

<If you want our bond to continue and strengthen, by all means keep using it,> he replied. *<You got that one wrong, by the way.>* Angela furiously erased the Pt she'd written as the chemical symbol for potassium. *<When we talked, the original bond scared you, much less the one we have now. You got lead wrong, too.>*

She erased that one too. *<What is lead's symbol?>* She asked.

<You know what it is. And gold's for that matter. Why DID you call me, Angela? You know the answers to all these.>

That made her pause; she wasn't deliberately sending the entire test to him. *<How are you doing that? Rummaging around my head and seeing through my eyes?>*

<I'm bored. Ms. Chen's still interrogating people who didn't do the summer reading,> he replied.

<Not answering my question,> she returned.

<True,> he paused. *<It's not so much a matter of rummaging or looking as paying attention to what's passing through your mind. The questions on your*

quiz are right there in the front of your mind. You DO know all the answers even if you're having trouble dredging them up from your deeper memory. Your frustration with it is clear. I suggest you breathe deeply and concentrate rather than ask me.>

She turned that over. *<Can you help me access my deeper memory?>*

She sensed his surprise. *<Angela, most of the power in this bond is on my end. For all the ease with which you're able to connect to me, I can do MORE with you. I'm pretty sure I can already take control of you, although you'd know I was doing it, and you can't do that to me. If the bond gets stronger, I might be able to do so without you being aware of it. We can't normally take control of someone for any longer than we're actually concentrating on doing it, at least not yet. Are you really sure you want to strengthen it in that way?>*

<Actually, Seth, I think I'd like to learn what you do. I want to be able to defend myself instead of relying on you or Bridget or Alex.>

That didn't surprise him. *<As I said in June, I'm not sure what we do can be taught. But if you're willing to learn, and you're sure you want to learn from me, and to put up with Teddy's comments, I'll give teaching a try.>*

<Teddy's comments?> She asked quizzically

<As someone learning from me? You can't hear him calling you the Angela of Death already?>

She snorted even as she finished the quiz. *<Well, I have heard people calling you the God of Death. I guess Alex wasn't able to hold the mystery in so well. So what do I need to do first, Your Holiness?>*

His voice came back quickly. *<First thing you'll need to do is study your ass off. I know Bridget mentioned that the more we know the more we can do. That really wasn't something she was repeating from her mother, although she certainly says it enough. Chemistry. Biology. Meteorology. Geology. Physics. Oh, and never ask for help this way on a test again. We don't cheat on tests.>*

<I get the idea. This is more involved than I thought.> Angela replied, but he continued on.

<And fantasy and science fiction. Imagination is about as important as knowledge in this. If not more important.>

<Okay, okay.>

<It's another three months before I'm allowed within fifty feet of you outside school, so you might as well begin the preliminaries.>

<You know this is kind of insane, right? You resurrected me a year ago. You spent the school year defending my mind from tampering. I spoke your name from miles away and you heard me. You saved my life in April and again in June. We're having this conversation entirely telepathically. And you're still not coming within fifty feet of me outside school>. She thought at him. <How am I supposed to learn this… OK, I know you and Jennifer don't like to call it this, but how am I supposed to learn magic from you if you won't even be in the same room with me?>

<Don't worry, you can handle it.> Seth thought back at her. <You just scored 100 on your quiz, > He obviously sensed her surprise. Then he continued.

<But the enlightenment of knowledge is only part of it. Do you truly wish to study with me? My path is one of death and darkness, Angela. I'm sure Bridget would be more than happy to teach you her powers of life and living things. Unlike any of the others, my powers are directly related to death and dying, killing and resurrecting. These abilities do not come without cost, Angela. None of them do, but mine weigh upon you heavily. The choice is yours, between light and dark. Make it wisely.>